Murder in

Tin

This is a work of fiction. Similarities to real people, places, or events are entirely coincidental.

MURDER IN MONTICELLO

First edition. September 22, 2024.

Copyright © 2024 Tim Lam.

ISBN: 979-8227914286

Written by Tim Lam.

Also by Tim Lam

Timeless Hearts
Ides of Love: A Journey to Ancient Rome

Standalone
Murder in Monticello

Table of Contents

The Triad 1
Suspicion 9
Cheating & Lies 16
The Investigation Begins 24
Harry Blakely 31
Marne's Tip 39
Cassie's Meeting 49
Panic Sets In 60
The Murder 75
Thanksgiving 87
The Affair 101
The Setup 111
The Smoking Gun 125
The Arrest 136
Kirk Hadley 148
The Trial 158
The Walls have Ears 170
Rick's Big Decision 182
The End of the Trial 195
Epilogue - Five Years Later 208

To my wonderful wife, Janice, without whose confidence in me this book would never have been written.

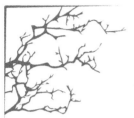

The Triad

The first rays of the new day edged their way over the tall pine trees surrounding the small town of Monticello, Georgia on this early spring morning. Like every morning, the spire atop the grey-domed courthouse was the first spot on the town square to feel the warm sunlight as it began to bathe this town of just over two thousand people. The two traffic lights on the square, and indeed the only two traffic lights in the county, signaled to the cars and trucks their permission to move on and off the square and send them on their way to their various destinations.

The courthouse opened at its usual time as the deputies manning the front door security checkpoint got ready for the day. It was a Friday, so magistrate court was the only court in session.

The three members of the "courthouse group", as they called themselves, began to filter in one by one. Judge Angelina Black, the state court judge, greeted the deputies as she walked around the metal detector on the way to her office.

Angelina was a tall woman in her mid-40s. She was in her third marriage, which she always told her friends was "the charm". She had worked at one of the local banks for years until the state court judge retired and she decided to run for that position. Her race was bitterly opposed by a retired attorney originally from Covington, a town just to the north of Jasper County, but her local connections were too much for him to overcome and she won by a landslide. She was about to open her door when she heard her name called from the opposite end of the hallway.

"Hey, Angelina, hold up." It was Louise Ambrose, the superior court clerk. "Are you free for lunch today?"

"Hey, Louise. Yeah, sure. Next door at that Amish place?"

"Sounds good. And they're Mennonite."

"Yeah, I always get those two confused," said Angelina.

"You say tomato, I say tomahto. Same thing," said Louise and the two women laughed.

Louise got on the elevator and headed directly to the magistrate judge's office, the place where she spent most of her workday. The magistrate judge, Cassie Manson, a pudgy woman in her late 30s, was divorced and never remarried nor had any children. Now in her third term as chief magistrate judge, she had been a deputy clerk in Louise's office for years, being assigned to the superior court criminal division. She had won her first election with the considerable help of a local church and her campaign had been one of the dirtiest in the county's history, accusing her opponent of being corrupt, billing for hours he didn't work, not collecting enough fines and a host of other things, all while as the deputy clerk that served her predecessor whom she was out to destroy. Many in the community wondered why Louise would allow her employee to say such things about the judge her office served. Most said things like "If I had been Cassie's boss I would have fired her ass immediately." But in truth, Cassie had been the real power in the clerk's office, dictating to Louise what duty she wanted to be assigned to and what hours she wanted to work. Louise was always more of a figurehead than an actual boss in her own office. That morning Louise walked into her friend's office to find her leaning back in her chair and staring out the window.

"You know, Louise, I'm thinking about changing these curtains. I think a brighter shade of blue would match the carpet better, don't you?"

"It's your office, Cassie. Change it however you want to, I say."

Cassie smiled and pointed out the window to the small parking lot below. "And you know, the sign on my parking space really needs to be painted. And I think I want my name on it this time too, Louise, instead of just 'Magistrate Judge'. The next time you see the county manager you will tell him about both of those things, won't you?"

"Sure. Hey, Angelina and I are having lunch next door today. You want to join us?"

"Yeah, girls' day out. Noon?"

"Yeah." Louise looked at the clock. "It's about time for your court, isn't it?"

"Yeah, let me go preside. Got to send all the bad guys to jail and throw out the trash tenants with evictions."

Magistrate court was called into session and Cassie took the bench with all the people standing. Once she had made them stand for a minute or so, even after she had sat down, she allowed them to sit. Her narcissism knew no limits.

She scanned the gallery of litigants awaiting their turn to plead their cases and particularly noted Aaron Ginn, a local real estate broker as well as many other things. Ginn had come from very humble beginnings to rise to prominence as one of the most important and influential black businessmen in the county. He had engaged in questionable business practices his whole life but he was very crafty at it, so he had never been investigated or charged with any crime.

Cassie could barely suppress a smile when Aaron came forward and presented his case for the eviction of Doris Abernathy, a widowed mother of three whose husband had recently been killed in a logging accident while high aloft in a stereotypical Georgia pine tree. The worker's compensation insurance carrier was balking at paying her because they raised the defense that he was a contractor and not an employee and therefore not entitled to worker's compensation coverage. She pleaded her eviction case in tears but the heartless Judge Manson had little sympathy, granting Mr. Ginn not only full possession of the mobile home, but giving her only three days to vacate instead of the usual seven and granting Ginn's request for back rent of over two thousand dollars with no proof whatsoever that she owed that much. He thanked the judge, picked up his copy of the judgment and left the courtroom to the sound of Ms. Abernathy and one of her children crying as they got on the elevator.

Cassie had always struggled to understand the legal terms and phrases thrown at her like a little leaguer playing catcher for the Atlanta Braves. Her predecessor, Christopher Harper, a highly-skilled and well-educated attorney in his late 40s with a doctorate in law, had no trouble presiding over cases with complex legal issues, but she had not a day of legal training in her life. She always kept a box of paper handkerchiefs in the top right drawer of the judge's bench for wiping the sweat off her brow that inevitably appeared about halfway through the day's calendar of cases.

But she had won the magistrate race over Harper very handily. Being a member of a local church had given her the votes she needed, but many wondered if the parishioners had ever thought through the consequences of having an incompetent judge on the bench and the effects her decisions would have not only on the people standing before her, but the many others who would feel the rippling effects of her bad legal decisions. How many would go to jail who shouldn't have? How many would be released from jail who should have stayed in? How many would lose their jobs, their homes, their families because she, with the stroke of a pen, unjustly ruined their lives?

But Cassie had managed to slug her way through court, feigning a look of listening intently to the arguments of the parties, especially those who had lawyers, often looking like the proverbial deer in the headlights when a fancy Latin phrase was thrown at her that she had neve heard before. She made a list of legal terms and phrases she had jotted down during the hearings so she could look them up after court, never letting those in attendance know that she had no idea what they were talking about. After the last case was heard she let out a sigh of relief, put the pack of handkerchiefs away - now with fewer tissues in it - and walked back to her office. Louise, who had returned to her own office shortly after magistrate court had gone into session, awaited the usual flood of parties coming in to appeal the wrong decisions her friend had just made upstairs.

Like her two other friends Louise Ambrose was a woman of hefty build which was offset in her appearance by her long blonde hair and pretty face. Now in her late 40s she had been a deputy clerk for some years before being the only one on the ballot for election to the position of Clerk of Superior Court, and she had won re-election several times afterwards. A wife and mother of two from a previous marriage, she was somehow able to balance her home life with her work life, but she made it clear to her husband, Rick, that her work came first, even at the expense of her family.

Just before noon the three women met in the hallway of the first floor and headed to the restaurant just outside the courthouse. They took their seats in a booth away from the other customers so they could talk freely. Their conversations were often not ones they wanted listening ears to hear. Each ordered her lunch and sat back comfortably after the waiter left their table.

"So," began Louise, "where are you two by now?"

"Well, I've collected about eleven thousand," replied Angelina. "What about you, Cassie?"

"I'm looking at close to fourteen thousand so far," said Cassie. "Louise?"

Louise looked at them, took a drink from her glass, set it down, smiled and said, "I'm at about nineteen thousand dollars."

"You go girl!" exclaimed Cassie.

The waiter returned to their table just as they were relishing in their accomplishments at embezzling from the county. He placed their mixed drinks on the table and left as they raised their glasses in a toast.

"To us," said Louise. "The best triad ever."

"What's a 'triad'?" asked Cassie.

"It means three of something, Cassie," answered Angelina. "Geez. Read a book."

"Hey, I'm the chief magistrate judge around here, lady," snapped Cassie jokingly. "I don't need to know big words or law or anything else as long as these morons keep re-electing me."

The three embezzlers shared a hearty laugh and took a drink from their large glasses of watered down mixed drinks as their loud voices caused some of the others in the restaurant to look their way.

"Yep. As long as we're in power, you don't need a dictionary," laughed Louise.

The other two nodded their heads in agreement as they made one last toast to finish off their drinks.

Sitting at a table across the restaurant was Marne Petakis, the head of Warriors for Citizens, the self-anointed local government overseer group, an association whose statement of intention is "dedicated to exposing corruption and overspending by government officials". In reality, Marne often used the cover of this organization, with its misleading banner of a public statement, to attack those in power and those seeking power from even coming into positions of importance with the county. She clothed herself in the good deeds she espoused to the citizens of the county and had gained a small but strong following, when in reality she was an autocrat, a suzerain, a would-be despot, a woman seeking not only to elevate herself in the eyes of the public but also to also destroy as many good public servants, and non-public servants for that matter, as possible in her quest. She had subtly orchestrated the outcomes of local elections, often paying people to run for office as a third candidate for the purpose of splitting up the vote enough to force a runoff, knowing that only a very small percentage of voters cast their ballots in runoffs and thus her candidate would have a better chance of winning. She often moderated public forums for candidates, meetings at which all candidates appear before a large room full of citizens to tout themselves, but despite describing herself as the "moderator" she regularly placed campaign signs for her favorite candidate in her yard and often had "plants" in the audience to ask questions of the candidates she opposed, while never asking or allowing even a single question of her own favorite candidate. A lonely, angry widow in her early-70s she had one child, a son who often distanced himself from her whenever he could.

As she sat at her table enjoying her roast beef sandwich she was careful to keep her face turned away from the three so as to not be recognized. But she had been able to hear bits and pieces of their conversation, just enough to pique her interest. She finished her meal and listened intently, but by now the noise of the lunchtime crowd was too loud for her to hear anything they were saying. The three finished their meals and, each by now feeling the effects of the three drinks they had each had, wobbled out of the booth and went back to the courthouse. Marne waited until they were out of sight, left the waiter a tip, paid her tab at the counter and left.

"I wonder what they're up to."

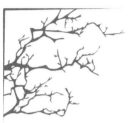

Suspicion

Benjamin Gillis, the county manager, returned to his office from his afternoon break to find Marne waiting for him in a chair just outside his door. He knew that her presence there always meant trouble, even if not necessarily for him. With her back to him as he walked to his desk he tilted his head back, rolled his eyes to the ceiling, took a deep breath and mustered "Good afternoon, Marne. What can I do for you today?"

"I wanted to file some public records requests, please." She reached into her oversized satchel and pulled out a stack of papers about half an inch thick.

"I see," sighed Benjamin. "So who is your target for today?"

"I don't have 'targets', Benjamin. I just want to see some records, that's all."

"OK. You'll get them within the mandated time, Marne."

"I'm sure I will. Thank you."

With that, Marne turned and left the manager's office, not so much as acknowledging Sheila Pounds, a county commissioner, who was walking in as Marne was walking out.

"What a bitch," she whispered to no one in particular, although Benjamin heard her clearly.

"Yes, she is," agreed Benjamin. "Well, let me go in here and see who she's after this week."

He sat down at his desk and looked over the requests. They were seeking the amounts received as fines for the magistrate court and state court, and the filing fees received by the clerk's office when new lawsuits are filed as well as other incoming fees for that office. He rubbed his chin and wondered why in the world Marne would be interested in such things, but then quickly remembered that he had long since stopped trying to figure out why Marne did anything she did.

THE NEXT MONDAY NIGHT found Marne up until after midnight poring over the financial records received from the county manager. She noticed that the fines in magistrate court had decreased considerably since the second and third Manson administrations had begun, down over 35% from her first administration. She turned to the state court records and saw the same trend during the same time period, the fines in that court being down about 28%. Then she saw that although civil lawsuit filings were up, the filing fees reported by the superior court clerk's office were also down by 24%. She then similarly compared the number of criminal cases disposed of in state and magistrate courts, and saw that the cases had actually increased in number.

"Hmmm. Interesting."

CASSIE ARRIVED AT THE appointed meeting place, the old Civic Center, a large, two-story building that once served as the school for the county's entire student population many years earlier. About a quarter of a mile off the square, it was the perfect place for the clandestine and illegal get togethers that had become such an important part of her administration as chief magistrate judge.

Judge Manson had come up with the idea while watching an old black-and-white movie one night early in her first term as chief magistrate. The plot about an attorney and a judge colluding together to shave portions of fines paid by those who pled guilty had struck her as something so simplistic she wondered why others in the courthouse hadn't thought of it before. You meet with the accused, have them pay a certain amount to you, then fine them a lower amount in court. What could be easier? And this way, unlike in the movie there's no need to involve lawyers or anyone else at all for that matter.

She had confided her scheme to her two closest friends during one of their hour and a half lunches one day shortly after she took office. At first they frowned upon the idea. But then it simmered in their minds, mulling through their brains over and over, until they caught themselves thinking about it all the time. Several weeks after she first told them about it they asked her for more details about how to do it without getting caught.

"Oh, it's easy," she had told them. "You just collect part of the fine from them, then in court fine them the difference. If their fine is, say, eight hundred dollars, you tell them that if they'll give you three hundred, you'll fine them only five hundred."

"But why do they agree to it?" asked Angelina. "I mean, what do they get out of it if the total amount they have to pay is the same either way?"

"That's the easy part. You just tell them you'll cut their probation time, or that you normally sentence people to jail for their offense but you'll suspend their jail time if they agree to do it your way, something like that. Believe me, I've been doing it for several months now and it's been working like a charm. You can't do it with everybody, of course, but you can pick out enough of these toothless trailer park types to get yourself a nice little stash. But you have to be real tough with them. You have to tell them that they're likely going to jail if they don't pay. These people are easily intimidated, especially by a judge. So you can't be Miss Nice Girl. Sometimes you've got to really chew some ass to make it work."

So began Cassie's life of crime. And her conversations with the other two convinced them to try their hands at it.

And they did. And it worked. Like a charm. So much so that all three were beginning to store up a notable amount of money, with no end to their scheme in sight.

Cassie was sure that she had perfected her method, a cat prowling the mouse's nest ready for the kill, experienced, patient, cunning. She had been in the Civic Center parking lot for about ten minutes when she saw a small Ford hatchback pull up, the passenger door a different color than the rest of the car, the rear bumper missing, and one taillight not working as it parked next to her car.

Out of the car stepped a short man, maybe 5'5", who looked like it would be a task for him to top the scales at a hundred pounds. He wore thick glasses that sat atop a nose that had obviously been broken more than once. He wore calf-length shorts that hung loosely on his legs, had brownish-gray hair that looked like it hadn't been washed in days and a tank top. He timidly shut the door and took a small step towards her.

"Judge Manson?"

"That's me. Are you Mr. Seabolt?"

"Yes, ma'am. You wanted to meet me to talk about my case?"

"That's right. I've got a proposition for you."

Her victim furrowed his brow in puzzlement, looked around from side to side, and asked, "Well, why here, judge? I mean, wouldn't the courthouse be the place to meet for this?"

"Who's the judge here, you or me?!" snapped Cassie as Mr. Seabolt recoiled back from her scolding. "This is a very routine matter, but our dealings must not be discussed with anyone. I'm giving you a break I don't give very many people. Now I want you to listen carefully to me, do you understand? You're charged with letting your dog run off your property and you failed to get him his shots for rabies."

"Uh, yes, ma'am, I know," answered Mr. Seabolt. "I think those are misdemeanors though, aren't they? I mean, I'm not looking at any jail time or anything, am I?"

"Don't tell me what the law is, Mr. Seabolt! I know what types of crimes they are! And I know that your ass certainly *can* land in jail for them, too!"

Mr. Seabolt stepped back at the judge's admonishment. Already apprehensive about coming to a face-to-face meeting with a judge to begin with, he was now panting in short breaths that his cigarette-strained lungs could hardly manage.

"Oh, yes, ma'am, I know I can. I don't mean any disrespect. I was just asking, that's all. I didn't mean anything, please, ma'am."

The judge lowered her voice a little at Mr. Seabolt's contrition. "That's more like it. Now, I think I have no choice but to sentence you to some time in the county jail, Mr. Seabolt. But I'm inclined to reconsider that if you'll pay your fine in a more informal manner."

"What does that mean?"

Cassie swiveled her head from side to side in one last look to make sure that they were completely alone. "You pay me four hundred dollars in cash and I'll cut your fine down to two hundred dollars and not order you to jail. And I'll reduce your probation time to six months instead of a year."

Mr. Seabolt, though uneducated and barely literate, saw the judge's meaning. He leaned back against his car, thought for a moment, and said, "OK. I can do that. But I've got your guarantee that I won't go to jail or be fined any more than two hundred dollars when we go to court? And no more than six months probation?"

"That's my promise, Mr. Seabolt. Do you have the money on you?"

"Lord, no, judge," replied Mr. Seabolt. "It'll take me a little while to come up with that much money."

"How much time do you need, Mr. Seabolt?"

"Can you give me a couple of weeks, maybe three? I've got a couple of odd jobs coming up, you know, painting, porch repairs, and so forth. I promise I'll do everything I can to get it all up as soon as possible."

"Well, court is the first Friday of next month. That gives you about three and a half weeks. You've got until the Wednesday before the court date. When you get the money together, call me at the courthouse office and let me know."

"Yes, ma'am. And thank you."

Cassie's answer was a short nod as she stepped back into her car and drove away. "Another one bites the dust," she said to herself as she made her way back to the courthouse. She smiled as she mentally added the money from this man to her stash that she had already bilked from the county. And its citizens.

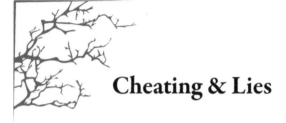

Cheating & Lies

State Court Judge Angelina Black drank her morning coffee in her office, sipping and smiling as she thought about the money she was stowing away. She had a meeting scheduled for that afternoon with a man charged with Driving Under the Influence who was set to appear before her the next month, a man with two DUIs already on his driving record and in peril of losing his driver's license for an extended period should he get another conviction.

The day passed quickly into the afternoon, and at 1:30 she told her staff that she had some business to tend to and would be out of the office for a while. She drove to the American Legion building, its World War II cannon pointing dutifully towards the east to ward off any attacks by armies approaching from neighboring Eatonton, its tires flat and the metal rusting from the years it had spent outside in the weather. She pulled into the gravel parking lot and waited for her next victim. A Cadillac, at least 50 years old, maneuvered its way into a parking space next to her car like a big fishing boat meandering its way through the waters of a bay to a dock. A black man, his hair white with age, fumbled with his walking cane as he struggled to hold the door open while he stepped out.

"Are you Judge Black?"

"I am. You're Mr. Blanton?"

"Yes, ma'am."

"Good. Now come over here and let's talk about your case."

The old man, well into his 70s, slowly propped himself up with the help of his cane and hobbled over to the judge's car. "Is there something going on with my case, judge?"

"Well, sort of. Mr. Blanton, I want us to talk about resolving your case in a way that won't hurt you too badly. I've got an idea how we can make that happen."

"That would be nice, young lady," replied Mr. Blanton.

"Don't call me that! I'm a judge. Show me the respect that my position calls for!"

"I'm sorry, ma'am," said Mr. Blanton as he recoiled at the judge's stern words. "I didn't mean nothing by it. Nothing at all. What did you have in mind?"

"Well, this is your fourth DUI in five years. If you're convicted, you're going to spend some time in jail, not to mention losing your driver's license for a while. Do you want that?"

"Oh, no, ma'am. I don't want to lose my license and I sho' don't want to go to no jailhouse, ma'am. That's the last place I want to go off to."

"Well then, maybe we can work something out. Your fine is two thousand dollars. But if you can give me a thousand, I'll reduce this to something like reckless driving and fine you five hundred more only. You won't lose your license that way. I won't even report it to the state for points against your driving record. Does that sound like something you'd be interested in?"

"Oh, yes, ma'am, that would be great!" exclaimed Mr. Blanton. "I don't need to go to no jail, no ma'am, no ma'am. I just want us to work this out, judge."

"OK, then. When can you come up with a thousand dollars?"

"I'll have to wait until my next gov'ment check comes in, but yes ma'am, I'll get it to you. Just please don't lock me up."

"You come up with it and I promise I won't. Then, after you pay me, you need to bring five hundred more to court for the rest of your fine."

With that, Judge Black turned and walked to her car, got inside, cranked the engine and drove away, leaving Mr. Blanton standing there alone. He shed a tear at the relief of knowing that he wouldn't have to go to jail if he could just come up with the money the judge demanded. He eventually put the end of his walking cane on the ground, took a deep breath, and shuffled to his car. Some falling leaves carried by the wind had gathered on his driver's seat through the open window, so he brushed them onto the ground, climbed inside and drove away.

THE SUPERIOR COURT clerk's office sat silent during the afternoon, not a particularly unusual occurrence for that office. Despite her budget being one of the highest of any office in the county, Louise had an overstaffed roster of workers, each one making a higher per hour rate of pay than any other employees in the courthouse. Her office workload was considerably lower than what she told the county commissioners and the public, but no one seemed to be able to do anything about it.

Over her time in office she had learned to maintain two sets of books, one with the actual figures for the office's revenues and another with figures that she turned in. Her "sweet book", as she called it, was the one in which she listed what was left from filing fees and other incoming monies after her hand sliced into it and took whatever share she felt she could embezzle without getting caught. Because of her slick bookkeeping she had managed to store up a handsome roll of cash for herself, with no one the wiser.

She closed the office at its usual time of 5:00 and drove home. Her husband, Rick, had called to say he was on his way, but as usual, she got home first. He had found out first hand that owning his own business meant that his hours weren't his, or his family's for that matter. And he was living proof of the old adage: "When you are self-employed, you have the worst boss you've ever had." She looked in the refrigerator and took out the thawed pork chops she had put in there the night before, got out the deep fryer, and began preparing supper. A few minutes later she saw the familiar sight of Rick's work truck driving up and turning into the driveway.

Rick arrived with his typical smile and a kiss for his wife, taking off his boots on the porch so as to not get mud on the carpet. His job as a landscaper often kept him busy until the sun went down, but this night he was home at around 6:00. He sat down in his favorite living room chair, opened up a beer, and reclined back to watch television, his white socks pointing up like two obelisks.

"When's supper gonna be ready?" he yelled.

"About half an hour. I'm going as fast as I can."

"All right," he said as he turned back to the TV.

The family sat at the dining table to eat their dinner. When they were finished the children went back outside to play before the setting autumn sun gave way to the darkness and Rick, having changed into some cleaner clothes and shoes, said that he had to go back to a job site to make sure that some sod had set.

"What do you mean?" asked Louise.

"Well, we put down some sod earlier today and watered it, and I just want to make sure that it's still in place because it's on a steep slope in the yard. I won't be all that long."

"You want us to ride with you?"

"No, there's no need for all that, Louise. Y'all just sit tight and I'll be back in a little while."

Louise nodded in reluctant agreement, kissed Rick goodbye and called the children inside to get their baths before bedtime which she watched Rick drive off in his four-wheel drive truck. However, Louise noticed that he turned to travel in a different direction than he had come from when he came home. Thinking little about it, however, she went into the bathroom, turned off the bathtub water, and began scrubbing the dirt from her little ones.

"DAMN, YOU'RE LATE. What happened? You couldn't get away?"

"I left as soon after supper as I could. Not as easy as you think. You don't have a spouse."

"Not yet," cooed Cassie as she wrapped her arms around Rick and kissed him passionately. "Remember what you promised."

"I know. I'll divorce her as soon as I can. But that's not as easy as you think either."

"Well, how much longer do you think it's going to take?"

Rick's answer was to grab Cassie's breasts and give them a squeeze, ending with a pinch of her right nipple. "Longer than it'll take to fuck your brains out."

Cassie laughed and the two headed to her bedroom.

MARNE PETAKIS ARRIVED for her meeting with Sheriff David Portis about ten minutes early. She was a very punctual woman, a trait reflected by her obsessive nature. She had gone through the courthouse records over and over and she was now sure that she had something that would be of interest to law enforcement.

In a few minutes the good sheriff opened the door. He was a fairly tall man, about 6'1", slender built with salt and pepper hair and a pair of glass that constantly sat about a third of the way down his long nose. He was a lifelong resident of Jasper County, born and raised there, with family roots that, even if not particularly possessed of great wealth, not only spread all across the county but far back to its early days of the county's original formation. In the eyes of the people he was one of the most popular sheriffs the county had ever had.

"Marne. So good to see you. Come on in, please."

"Thank you for seeing me, Sheriff, especially on such short notice."

"Oh, never too busy to see you, Marne. Have a seat. Can I get you a cup of coffee, water?"

"No, thank you, I'm fine. I'm here to let you know that I have found some discrepancies in the financial records at the courthouse, particularly the state and magistrate courts and the clerk's office."

"Oh?"

"It seems that more fines should have been collected than have been, Sheriff. The number of people being fined has increased, but not the fines collected. There should be a correlation between the two, but there's not. In fact, the fines are actually down. And the number of civil case filings has increased, but not the filing fees and other incoming fees that should have been collected by the clerk."

"Well, what are you suggesting, Marne?"

"I don't want to make accusations, Sheriff, but I think you should look into the reason for the lack of increase in the amounts collected. Since more people are being fined and filing civil suits, I don't understand why the money collected have been so low compared to previous years. It's particularly noticeable with the magistrate court, but the trend is also apparent with the state court. I am at a loss as to why somebody was fined eight hundred dollars in the past and they're only fined three or four hundred dollars now for the same offenses. It just seems strange to me."

"Are you suggesting some wrongdoing on the part of the two judges and the clerk?"

"At this point, Sheriff, I don't know what I'm suggesting. But I have the records and figures. Here," she said as she handed the stack of papers to the Sheriff.

"OK, Marne. I'll look into it. But keep in mind that neither I nor anyone else can tell judges what to fine people. It might just be that they're working out plea deals that call for lower fines than in the past."

"I understand, Sheriff. I'm just asking you to take a look into it."

"That I'll do, Marne. Is there anything else I can help you with?"

"No, thank you. I appreciate your time."

The Investigation Begins

The next few weeks passed with the self-described "triad" of corrupt women continuing to work their scheme to perfection. Many defendants in the state and magistrate courts paid money to the judges, always cash, and saw their fines reduced, the charges reduced or even dismissed. The clerk of court also skimmed money from fines being paid for magistrate court cases and filing fees for new cases being filed. The three were beginning to see their once-meager stashes get larger and larger, topping first twenty thousand dollars, then twenty-five, then over thirty thousand for each of them.

But for one of them, while things with her embezzling operation was going very well, Louise had begun to notice something at home that was, well, different. Her husband, Rick, left earlier and earlier for work each morning, came home later and later, and he seemed aloof and distant when he was there. And there were those trips back to the job sites after supper that became more and more frequent. One night while Louise was washing the dinner dishes he made his usual comments about having to go back to a job site, this time something about checking on some grass seeds that had been scattered right before the rain, and Louise decided to press him.

"Why do you have to go back out there tonight, Rick? I mean, what's so special about grass seeds?"

"If they're not covered with hay they'll wash away at the first drop of rain, Louise. I've got to go make sure there's enough hay scattered over it so that it doesn't."

"Well, why didn't you do that before you left there?"

"Not enough time. I knew you were cooking and I didn't want to be late for supper."

"Where're you going, daddy?" It was the voice of Rick's youngest step-daughter, Elena, who had just turned four and who, like the other two children, had called Rick "daddy" from the beginning.

"Oh, daddy's got to go to the job site and make sure everything's all right, honey. If it rains all the grass seeds will wash away."

Louise coldly kissed Rick and he hurriedly walked to his truck, wasting no time in leaving her and the children standing in the living room, waving through the window. He smiled and waved back.

The next day at work Louise sat at her desk staring out the window. She was startled out of her thoughts when Cassie lightly tapped on her door and walked in.

"Oh, hey, Cassie. I'm sorry. I guess I was daydreaming."

Cassie laughed and took a seat. "Something on your mind?"

"Oh, it's just Rick. He's been acting awfully strange lately. Coming home late, then always going back out after supper to check on some job site. Just strange."

Cassie swallowed hard and tried not to show any reaction. "Well, I guess in his line of work he has to check on stuff from time to time, especially since he owns his own business now. You don't think there's anything going on with him, do you?"

"No, not really. He just seems to be acting weird lately, that's all."

"Well, men. What can I say?"

"Yeah," chuckled Louise. "I guess you're right."

"How about we get with Angelina and have lunch today? It's specials on drinks at our usual place."

"Yeah, sounds good."

CASSIE RETURNED TO her office and closed her door, then decided to call her boyfriend by phoning Matt, his employee. She knew better than to call Rick's cell phone on which Louise could easily see any recent calls on his screen. She asked for Rick and Matt handed the phone to Rick where he heard Cassie's worried voice.

"I just had lunch with Louise. I think she's getting suspicious, Rick. She said that you've been acting strange at home lately. We need to meet at some time other than after you've gotten home at night. I'm afraid she's going to find us out."

Rick walked away from the other workers for more privacy. "Oh, Cassie, you've got nothing to worry about, believe me. She won't find out. Just sit tight and let me get to the point where I can get the divorce started."

"Rick, you promised me that months ago! I'm getting a little impatient with all this. Now, you've got to do something soon or we're through. I'm not going to be involved in some scandal because of you. It could cost me the next election. I'm not going to lose this cushy job because of you or anybody else!"

"Cassie, calm down, will you? Nobody's going to lose their job and nobody's going to get caught. Let's just keep doing what we're doing for now and I promise you, I'll get the divorce started when the time is right."

Cassie shrugged and rolled her eyes. "Well, it'd better be soon."

"Don't worry. It will be."

"Soon."

"Cassie, I've got to get back to work now, OK? Just relax and everything'll work out. It really will."

"Well, you'd better step up your timetable, Rick. That's all I've got to say."

Cassie then abruptly ended the call. Rick stood with the phone to his ear for several seconds, rolled his eyes to the sky and handed Matt's phone back to him.

"Everything all right, Rick?" asked Matt.

"Yeah, fine. Just women, you know. Thanks for taking the call. That was important; one of my former customers who needs something else done to her yard. My cell phone battery is dead."

"No problem," laughed Matt.

SHERIFF PORTIS SAT in his favorite recliner after supper and laid the stack of courthouse records across his lap. There were ledgers, spreadsheets, balance sheets, financial statements, columns of figures that seemed to go on forever. The sheriff took a gulp of his ice tea, rubbed his eyes and in a low voice said to no one in particular, "Well, gotta get started sometime."

The sheriff went over the figures provided him by Marne Petakis. At first he was skeptical about her suspicions. He had known all of the principals that she suspected for years and had no reason to think that they would ever be involved in anything unethical, much less illegal. But as he went further into the records he began to see a pattern emerge. More defendants, more convictions, but less money collected for fines; more lawsuits filed in superior court, but less money collected for filing fees and certain items. His extensive background as a law enforcement officer guided his analysis. He examined the figures. He did some simple math. He added, subtracted, multiplied, divided. He began to grow more and more suspicious. Finally, at around 10:30 that night his wife walked downstairs and saw him still sitting in his chair with the light glaring down upon him from the table beside him.

"What're you going over, David?"

"Oh, just some financial figures in a case we're working, honey." He never liked to involve his wife in his work. Besides, as the sheriff's wife and a longtime resident of Jasper County herself she knew all three of the women Marne suspected. The last thing he needed was for her to know something that if disclosed could compromise a case he's working on, even unintentionally.

Sheriff Portis continued thumbing through the pages of financial records, making notes, using post-its with little abbreviations written on them, furrowing his brow from time to time when he saw some figures that seemed to strike him as something that perhaps, just perhaps, the town busybody might be right about. She had made so many false accusations against so many innocent people in the past that in the people's minds her name had become synonymous with the story of the boy who cried wolf.

But this time appeared to be different. His suspicions grew, something that was not particularly common for him. Despite being the chief law enforcement officer of the county he was unusually skeptical, or at least openminded, when he conducted an investigation sparked by someone's bare allegation that a person was committing a crime, especially when the person pointing the finger was Marne. Throughout his career he had often parted company with many of his brothers and sisters in blue who had a habit of just charging and anybody when they had the least suspicion about their involvement in a crime. Sheriff Portis had made a point of keeping his frame of mind focused on truly investigating and then drawing conclusions, not the other way around. That way, if he was honestly convinced that the suspect was guilty, he would have no trouble swearing out an arrest warrant and bringing him or her to justice. But his conscience would not allow him to charge someone who might have been at the wrong place at the wrong time or simply been somewhere on the premises when someone else was really the guilty party.

So he kept reading, adding and subtracting. He noted that the number of defendants brought before both magistrate and state courts had steadily increased over the past months while sure enough, the amounts collected in fines steadily declined.

"Hmmm."

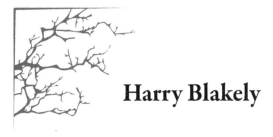

Harry Blakely

Louise served the last plate of spaghetti to Rick and the children without saying a word. The atmosphere in that house had been a bit different lately with Louise rolling her husband's recent behavior over and over in her mind. Is he having an affair? she wondered. Is there some problem at work that's got him distracted? Is he having some sort of medical issue that he doesn't want to talk about?

These ideas festered in her mind for the next several days. She pondered his lack of attention to her, his leaving the house after supper practically every night to check on some job site, even his distant attitude towards the children.

But it was now Thursday and in all fairness to him, she reasoned, he had not left out after supper any day that week. Louise began to relax a little in her suspicions. She asked everyone if they wanted to go to Dairy Queen for an ice cream.

"Sounds good," said Rick.

The Ambrose family walked into the Dairy Queen, busy with the middle school football game crowds coming in for their night of supper out or something for a sweet tooth. Louise was surprised to see Cassie at a booth drinking a milkshake.

"Hey," she shouted. "Y'all come on over here and sit with me."

"Sounds good," replied Louise. "Let us get our stuff and we'll be right over."

The group moved to a bigger table, one that would accommodate all of them.

"How's it going?" asked Cassie.

"Just coming in for an ice cream. We've already had supper."

"So, how have you been, Rick?" asked Cassie. "It's been a while."

Rick could hardly suppress his uneasiness at the entire situation and Cassie's remark. It hadn't been a while. It hadn't even been a short while. It had been the day before when he took the company truck to pick up some piping in Greensboro, stopping by Cassie's house just long enough to give her his pipe during her lunch hour, which always turned into lunch hours.

"Oh, just fine, Cassie. Working too damn hard. Always something to do. But I guess that's the way it is when you're the boss, huh?" Rick managed a laugh despite his discomfort at all of them sitting at the same table.

"Yeah," interjected Louise, "I'm about ready to divorce his ass if he doesn't get more employees so he won't have to work so long himself. It seems like practically every night after supper he has to go back out to check on some job site."

Rick turned white at Louise's remark. But it delighted Cassie to no end to see him squirm.

"Typical woman's bullshit," he thought to himself.

MARNE SAT IN HER HOME office where she worked as an financial advisor and, after making sure that it was past 5:00, got out the stack of papers she had been given by the county manager, spread them out on her desk, and once again began to go over them. She had found many discrepancies in the amounts of fines collected when compared to the number of defendants before the magistrate and state courts. When more people are assessed fines, more money should be collected, right? That only makes sense. Common sense. And she couldn't wrap her head around how not only did fine totals not increase, or even stay the same, but actually decreased.

And one more thing caught her attention. There had been more reductions of charges and outright dismissals than ever before. Almost nobody was convicted or pled guilty to what they were originally charged with in either the magistrate or state court. In state court there were practically no guilty pleas or convictions of driving under the influence, almost all of them being reduced to reckless driving.

And the magistrate court cases were really no different. Where people once paid fines of five, six, seven hundred, a thousand, fifteen hundred dollars, now they were paying two, three, four hundred dollars. Why were the fines reduced so? There should be thousands more collected in fines, she thought. No, she knew there should be. She was certain.

She had to meet with the sheriff again.

THE DEFENDANT, HARRY Blakely, sat nervously in his chair at counsel's table in the main courtroom of the Jasper County Courthouse while the jury was in the jury room deliberating. These lulls in activity during the trial had proven to be the most stressful times for him, a man charged with murder that he swore he hadn't committed. A small crowd had gathered in the audience for most of the trial, with more people joining as it neared its conclusion. His attorney, Royceland Kane, an older and highly-respected attorney whose family's roots go all the way back to the early days of the county, smiled and exchanged jokes with the sheriff and Jamie Clinton, the district attorney and Danyale Jones, the assistant D.A., making Blakely nervous. He had seen Mr. Kane being friendly with all of the players on the opposite side of his team, but he never understood how you could oppose someone professionally and not be at odds with them personally, like the lawyers are in movies and television shows.

"We're opponents, not enemies," Mr. Kane had explained to him. "I go way back with many of the people on the state's side, even the judge. Hell, Judge Partridge and I grew up together, went all the way through school together. And Jamie and I sometimes have a drink of Jack Daniels together in my office after hours. We're friends and have been for many years. But that doesn't stand in my way of doing the very best I can for my clients, including you."

And in truth, he had done a good job. No, he had done a great job. It was no wonder to Blakely that Mr. Kane, "Royce" to his friends, had such a reputation and list of clientele in this small town. It seemed like there was no one in the entire county who didn't know him or hadn't been represented by him. And he seemed to win. And win. And win. Practically always. The quintessential prevailing attorney in the sea of legal battles, always firing the killing blow from the bow of his ship to shatter the hull of his attacker's ship. And he always seemed to win.

He was an attorney from the old school. Not flamboyant, nor showy, nor colorful. Not loud, no, not loud at all. In fact, in normal conversation one had to listen carefully to even hear everything he was saying. He didn't pound the podium with his fist, sweat profusely, wave his arms, raise his voice, quote the Bible or Shakespeare. No, not Royceland Kane.

He just won. And won.

His mind was a walking encyclopedia of legal knowledge. He was a fairly tall man, slim and well-dressed. Always well-dressed. He didn't buy his suits anywhere but fine clothing stores. He had his clothes tailor-made to fit perfectly. His shirts were always professionally dry-cleaned and pressed, as were his suits. His salt-and-pepper hair reflected his years of experience as an attorney. His shoes were shined like a military man's at inspection. He stood up straight, never hunching over despite being over 70 years of age. His demeanor was always one of overt friendliness to all others, even those he opposed. Often attorneys visiting from big cities, where they were accustomed to opposing counsels being boorish, surly, sometimes even downright rude, were surprised at his congenial personality and his smiles and handshakes when he met them.

But he had the financial status to be different if he had wanted to be. A millionaire several times over, he could have easily been a real jerk if he were so inclined. Yes, he could afford to be prudish . . . but he wasn't. That wouldn't be his nature.

He was a friendly man, that's who and what he was. Many were the times he stood around waiting for court to convene, talking and laughing with the other lawyers, then asking who wanted a fresh cup of coffee from the restaurant on the opposite side of the town square. When he returned with a cupholder filled with steaming cups, he adamantly refused to accept any money from anyone. That was just Royce.

But he tried cases to win them, to be sure. Now nearing the end of his career, he had compiled a box score that would rival the best lawyers in the biggest cities in Georgia, or anywhere in the United States, for that matter.

And this was one case of many in which he had presented a defense that was impeccably perfect. A man accused of murder who had insisted from the beginning that he was innocent. He said that he was not there when the murder was committed, knew nothing about it, had no idea what had happened to the poor lady who had once been his girlfriend.

But Jamie Clinton and Danyale Jones were sure they had an air-tight case. Mr. Blakely had ridden his bicycle from Shady Dale to Monticello, about eight miles away, on a lightly-traveled highway, even less traveled in the middle of the night, with no street lights and sparsely-spaced houses in between, with no lights on his bike, then stopped in the victim's yard and took his rifle, which he had somehow brought with him on his two-hour bike ride, tip-toed up to the victim's bedroom window, pointed the rifle through the window into the unlit bedroom, shot the victim, then managed to ride back to his home in Monticello in the same fashion in which he had ridden up there, with no one seeing him along the way going either direction.

Yes, said Clinton to himself, this is a good case, a great case. I can get this man convicted and justice will be served. Justice hand-delivered to the poor victim, to her family, to her friends, to the community . . . to everyone.

But Mr. Kane had other ideas. His brilliant presentation and cross-examinations of the state's witnesses had chipped away at the brick wall of certainty Jamie Clinton had, or thought he had. Then came the knock on the jury room door. Mr. Blakely sat up straight at the sound of the knock, fidgeting and squirming in his chair.

The bailiff opened the door and was handed a note from the foreman of the jury. She immediately brought the note to the judge, who was in his chambers relaxing and damn near asleep, that the jury had a note to deliver to him and which she handed to His Honor. The judge sat up straight in his chair, wiped his eyes and read the note, then looked at the bailiff.

"Gather everybody up."

"Yes, sir."

The entire courtroom was soon assembled, the bailiffs, the attorneys, the defendant Mr. Blakely, the court reporter, even the courtroom spectators all in place.

"We're now back on record in the case of State of Georgia v. Horace Blakely. I have received a note from the jury that reads, 'We have reached a verdict.' Bailiff, please bring the jury back into the courtroom."

The bailiff did as she was told and within a few minutes the jury was seated.

"Ladies and gentlemen, I have received a note from you that you have reached a verdict. Will the foreman or madame foreman please stand?"

A short man with white hair stood.

"Are you the elected foreman of the jury?"

"I am."

"Has the jury reached a verdict?"

"We have, Your Honor."

"Please hand the verdict to the clerk of court. Ms. Ambrose, please publish the verdict."

Louise took the verdict from the jury foreman and read it out loud. "We, the jury, find the defendant not guilty."

A sigh went out through one part of the courtroom while others groaned in disgust.

"Mr. Blakely, please stand and face me. You have been duly tried and found not guilty by a jury of your peers. You are free to go."

Louise resumed her seat in the clerk's chair next to the judge's bench after reading the verdict.

"Not guilty, my ass," she mumbled.

Marne's Tip

Marne Petakis left the courtroom after the trial of Harry Blakely just as disgusted as that portion of the spectators made up of the victim's family and friends. She felt that an injustice had been done to the fine citizens of Jasper County, the same citizens whose lives she indiscriminately destroys whenever she can. There was never any rhyme or reason for her attacks or the motives she had for making them. She was like Caesar – she simply points her mighty finger out over her domain, waves it back and forth until it stops on the one she wants to crucify that day, and she has her next victim in her sights. Then she becomes obsessed with making it happen. She always did it under the guise of looking out for the people of the county, of making it a better county for all to live and work in.

But it never seemed to result in that happening. She managed to inflict a great deal of hurt and pain on so many people, some deserving of it and some not. But what did she care? Whether she was justified or not, whether her actions were noble or not, whether she was right or wrong did not matter to her. It only mattered that her target went down the way she wanted it to.

She saw Sheriff Portis leave the courtroom after the trial amid the usual mingling and handshaking. She had analyzed enough of those financial records to know that something was wrong, terribly wrong. She decided to make another visit to the Sheriff's Department.

"SHERIFF PORTIS, THERE'S someone here to see you," informed Jenny Kirkland, the sheriff's secretary through the speaker.

"Name?" replied the sheriff.

"Marne Petakis."

"Thank you. Send her in."

"Good to see you, sheriff. Thank you for seeing me without an appointment."

"It's my pleasure, Marne. I saw you in the courtroom earlier. That was some trial, huh?"

"Some miscarriage of justice, if you ask me."

"Now, Marne, the system gave both sides their fair trial and the jury found him not guilty. We can't be any more critical when someone is acquitted who we think is guilty than we can be when an innocent person gets convicted, which sometimes happens. We have to accept all verdicts no matter how we see them and whether we agree with them or not."

"I know, I know. I just hate to know that a murderer is walking our streets."

"He's not a convicted murderer. Remember?"

Marne shrugged as if the jury's verdict meant no more to her than when she destroys the life and career of someone who has done nothing wrong other than to have found himself or herself in the bullseye of Marne's target, or at the end of her bony pointed finger.

"Anyway, I was just checking in to see if you had had a chance to review any of the financial records I brought to you the other day. I've been going over them myself and I must tell you, I found a lot of things to be suspicious about."

"Yes, Marne, I've been going over them and yes, there are some things that I want to look further into. But there are a lot of figures in there and it's going to take a little while to digest them all. So just sit tight and be a little patient, OK, like I asked you before. If there's something being done that's not above board, I'll get to the bottom of it, believe me."

"I hope you can, sheriff. And I appreciate your attention to all this."

Marne then shook the sheriff's hand, her grip as tight as any man's, which always made him cringe as soon as her back was turned. He sat back down at his desk, thought for a moment and said to himself, "It's time for a meeting."

SHERIFF PORTIS CALLED the cell phone of Cassie Manson, preferring not to call her on her office phone. The screen told her who was calling.

"Hello there, sheriff. How'd the trial turn out today? I haven't been out to see anybody who was there, but I went to lunch and the courtroom was empty so I knew it was over."

"They let him go, judge. I guess Jamie just didn't have quite the case he thought he had. But then again, Royce is hard to beat, one of the best. The very best."

"Well, my condolences, sheriff. I know you and your department put a lot of time and effort into that case."

"Thank you. Say, judge, would you be available for a meeting sometime today? I've got something I'd like to go over with you, if you don't mind."

"Sure. What's on your mind, sheriff?"

"Just something I'd like to discuss with you. I'll try not to take up too much of your time."

Cassie found herself reaching for that other box of tissues she kept in her desk drawer.

"What time?"

"Is now a good time?"

"Sure, no problem. Come on over."

"See you in a few minutes."

The two hung up and Cassie immediately called Angelina at the state court.

"Angelina, the sheriff is on his way over here. He called and said that he wanted to talk about something with me but he wouldn't say what it was over the phone. I'm beginning to get a little nervous, Angelina. You don't think he's on to any of us, do you?"

"Cassie, calm down. I'm sure it's nothing. Don't you talk to the sheriff and his deputies all the time?"

"I do, but they're never so cagey about what they want to talk about. They'll usually say that they've got a search warrant they want me to sign, or ask about somebody's bond conditions that I've set, or something like that. And seldom do they want to talk in person. But David wouldn't say a word about why he wants to meet. Nothing."

"Well, just keep your wits about you. We'll have a good laugh after he leaves and you see that he was just wanting to ask you to revoke somebody's bond or something."

Cassie let out a long, deep breath. "I'll try."

She was sitting at her desk, trying to calm down and staring out the office window at her assigned parking space with her name on the placard when she heard the sheriff speaking to her secretary. She opened her office door with a big fake smile and said, "Sheriff, please come on in."

"Thank you."

"Can I get you anything? Cup of coffee?"

"No, thank you, I'm fine," he replied as he swung the large bundle of papers out from under one arm into the other in anticipation of taking a seat. Cassie took her chair behind her large desk as if it were some sort of a shield from the lawman.

"So what's on your mind, sheriff?"

"Judge, I've been looking over some of your court's records, uh, fines, fees, restitution, numbers of defendants, and so forth. Some questions have come up about the amounts of money that have been taken in compared to the numbers of people who are paying them, and the average amounts of the fines you're assessing. Now, let me make it perfectly clear here and now that I fully recognize that each judge sets the fines as he or she sees fit. There's no disagreement about that at all. You are free to assess any fine that the law allows in any case if that person pleads guilty or is found guilty. But, uh, judge, it's been noticed that the average fine amounts are a bit lower than they've been in the past. If I may ask, judge, have you adopted a policy of assessing lower fines these days?"

"Well, in some cases the fines that my predecessor levied did seem a bit high, sheriff, so there have been some slightly lower fines imposed recently. I'm sure that's where the discrepancies appear."

"I didn't say there were any discrepancies."

Cassie stared at him in silence. After a few seconds that seemed like hours, she spoke.

"Well, maybe that's not the right word, sheriff," she nervously laughed. "I mean, I, I, well, I suppose I meant the differences between what fines I assess compared to what my predecessor used to assess. And they're all paid directly into the court through the usual channels. I don't handle any of it personally."

The sheriff's puzzled face made Cassie break eye contact with him.

"Well, I wasn't asking about who personally collects them, judge. I was just curious about the amounts."

"Oh, of course, sheriff. They're all there, in black and white," she said as she pointed to the sheriff's stack of papers.

"Well, I appreciate your time, judge," said the sheriff as he gathered up his papers and stood up.

"My pleasure, David."

The sheriff exchanged pleasantries with the judge's secretary and left the magistrate office. Cassie sat back down at her desk, breathed a heavy sigh, and propped her forearms on her desk with her chin in her hands.

"That goddamn Marne Petakis."

"GOOD MORNIN', MISS Marne," greeted Sam Echols as he put gas in his riding lawn mower in the yard of his long-time client.

"Good morning, Sam," returned Marne. "I guess this'll probably be your last time cutting the grass for this year, won't it?"

"Yes, ma'am, I suppose it will. I was hopin' that there might be some other things I could do around here during the off-season like I did last year. I'll be glad to keep the leaves raked up and the hedges trimmed for ya."

"I feel sure I can use you some during the winter, Sam."

"I'd appreciate that, Miss Marne. I'm gonna have a pretty big ticket to pay off in a few days so I can use all the work I can get."

"Really, a ticket? What happened?"

"Oh, I've got a pretty big mess in my yard that I've been tryin' to get cleaned up, but it's just takin' a while and the county code officer wrote me a ticket for it. I've got court in a couple of weeks."

"Oh my goodness, Sam. I'm sorry about that. Do you know how much the ticket's supposed to be?"

"Well, it's pretty big, but I think I might be able to work somethin' out with the judge. She wants to meet me tomorrow mornin' to talk about it."

"No, Sam, you mean Monday? Today's Friday."

"No, ma'am, it's tomorrow."

"You're meeting with the judge on a Saturday? The courthouse isn't even open on Saturdays."

"Well, we're meetin' somewheres else, Miss Marne," replied Sam, his thick rural Southern accent almost too difficult for anyone other than another southerner to understand. Marne had tried to help him know that there's no such word as "somewheres" before, but forty-five years of speaking the same dialect apparently couldn't be broken.

"Well, that's odd. Anyway, let me know what you want for lunch in enough time to fix it for you, Sam."

"I appreciate that, Miss Marne, I always appreciate that."

Sam then got on his mower, cranked it and began cutting the autumn lawn as Marne went back into her home office to begin working. She sat for a couple of hours doing her computer work while Sam worked outside. But Sam's statement about meeting the judge on a Saturday morning to discuss his case continued to bug her throughout the morning. Finally, she heard a soft tap on her door.

"Miss Marne?"

"Yes, Sam."

"One of yo' grilled cheese sandwiches would be great, if'n you don't mind, Miss Marne."

"Grilled cheese it is, Sam."

About twenty minutes later Sam washed up at the outdoor spigot and came inside, first taking off his hat in respect to "Miss Marne". He sat down at her dining room table and the two ate together. He was always impressed at how Marne, even with her hated reputation around the town, had treated him so well. Maybe it was because he seemed so down on his luck all the time. Maybe it was because he was such a hard worker who had kept her lawn and surroundings looking so well. Maybe it was because he had never asked for a raise. Or maybe it was just because he had no worldly ambitions and therefore would never venture into the county's limelight and thus would never be someone whom she would target to bring down. At any rate, he thanked her profusely for the sandwich and ice tea and took his seat.

"Sam, tell me more about this ticket. You say it's for a county ordinance violation?"

"Yes, ma'am, I think that's what they call it. The lady said it's not a state law or anything."

"'The lady', you mean the county code enforcement officer?"

"Yes, ma'am, I think that's what they call her." Then he laughed. "I just call her 'ma'am'!"

"When is your court date?"

"Uh, December 6th, I think it is."

Marne reached for a calendar. "Uh, let's see . . . that's a Friday, so it must be magistrate court. That's what I figured. They handle code enforcement matters."

"Yes, ma'am, I think that's it."

"And your meeting with the judge, how did that come about to be set up?"

"Well, I got a call from a lady who said she's the judge and she wanted to see if I was willin' to work somethin' out about my ticket. She said the fine is a thousand dollars but if I'd pay half of that up front in cash, she'd reduce the rest to three hundred. She said it's some sort of new program to help keep points off people's driver's licenses."

Marne cocked her head. "Uh, Sam, you don't get points assessed against your driver's license for having a messy yard. That's usually only for driving violations. Why would the judge tell you that?"

"I don't know, Miss Marne. I'm just tellin' you what she told me."

"Well, that doesn't make any sense, Sam. Tell me, where are you supposed to meet her?"

"Out on Armour Road."

"Armour Road? What time?"

"That's what's a little weird, Miss Marne. She wants to do it at 7:00."

"Seven o'clock in the evening?

"No, ma'am. Seven o'clock in the mornin'."

Where on Armour Road did she say?"

"Where it intersects with Wehunt Road."

"Okay. Well, enjoy your sandwich, Sam."

"Thanks again, Miss Marne. It's delicious."

Cassie's Meeting

The late-November Saturday morning brought a real chilliness and crispness to the air. Cassie drove to the designated spot on the dirt road several miles outside town, becoming more and more agitated at the hunters that invade her county every fall in search of that record buck. The annual Deer Festival had been held a few Saturdays before and she confessed that she did enjoy going to it, but she always dreaded the influx of "ferners", the locals' moniker for the out-of-towners that was a corruption of the word "foreigners". It was a further drive than she usually made to meet her victims, but after the sheriff's visit she was more wary than she had been before. She was sure that meeting way out here would keep her from the prying eyes of not only the sheriff but Marne Petakis and anyone else who might see her with her next victim.

She stopped at the intersection of Armour and Wehunt Roads and parked. There are precious few houses on those roads and at that hour no one was stirring about, just the way she planned it. She nervously awaited the arrival of her next source of "cash for my stash", as she called it. Sure enough, at around five after seven, with the sun still low in the autumn sky, she saw a broken down pickup truck drive up Armour Road and stop. It was Sam Echols.

"Hey, judge?" asked Sam as he got out of his truck.

"Yes, I'm Judge Manson. Are you Mr. Echols?"

"Yes, ma'am."

"Come on over here."

Sam did as he was told and the two stood beside her car.

"Mr. Echols, do you have the cash we talked about?"

"Yes, ma'am, I do." Sam reached into his pocket and counted out five one hundred dollar bills and handed them to Cassie. "What do we do from here?"

"Well, as I explained on the phone, you come to court next month, I'll reduce your fine to three hundred dollars, and this five hundred will be applied to your Points Elimination Register. That way you won't lose your driver's license."

"Yes, ma'am. But can I ask you one question, please, ma'am?"

"What is it?"

"I was told that you don't get points against your license for this kind of charge, only driving crimes."

Cassie became livid. "What?! Are you questioning what I'm telling you, Mr. Echols?! Who's the judge here, you or me?! Do you want me to just give you this money back and have you arrested for contempt of court? How dare you question what I can do in my own court!"

Sam put his hands up in a submissive gesture and took a couple of steps back. "Oh, no ma'am, no ma'am, I didn't mean nothin' like that at all, no ma'am. I just heard that somewheres, that's all."

"Where did you hear that from, Mr. Echols? Did you ask a lawyer? Huh? Or did one of your hick friends tell you that?"

"Oh, no ma'am, it was Miss Marne, a lady I cut grass for told me."

"Miss Marne? Marne who?"

"Uh, Marne Pekata, Packata, somethin' like that. I can't quite pronounce her last name, judge."

Cassie froze when she realized who Sam was talking about. Sam's poor attempt at saying her last name was still enough to inform her who he was talking about. This man cuts her grass? Had he told her about the ticket? Had he told her about how she would keep points off his driver's license if he would pay a portion of his fine directly to her in cash? Oh my god, she thought. What all did he tell her? She stood for a moment, swallowed hard, and lowered her voice.

"Well, I tell you what, Mr. Echols. This entire meeting is just between us. I'm going to do you a big favor and go ahead and help you with your case, but I can tell you right now that I don't like one bit you questioning me about all this and asking others questions about it either. I was just trying to help you out and you've made me think twice about doing it, but I guess you just didn't know any better. So I'm going to go ahead and do what I said I would do, but you can't mention our meeting or how you paid part of your fine to me to anyone else, do you understand? That Points Elimination Register is a really good thing and you ought to let me help you out by taking advantage of it. Now get back in your car and go."

"Yes, ma'am, thank you so much, judge."

Cassie nodded as the hapless Sam drove away, no more aware that he had been conned than when he first arrived. A poor, uneducated man who could barely read and write, he was a prime target for Cassie, someone unlikely to make any trouble for her if she exercised enough overbearing authority over him.

But Marne. Yes, Marne. Now that was a problem. A big problem. That nosy bitch could really throw a wrench into her well-oiled machine. A big, heavy, solid metal wrench. A wrench that could disrupt not only Cassie's little enterprise but one that could cause a rippling effect for Angelina and Louise too.

Cassie stood leaning up against her car for a few minutes, thinking about the situation.

Screw Angelina and Louise. If things go wrong it's every woman for herself. And right now Cassie was the only one whose name, as far as she knew, had been mentioned to Marne or anyone else. She slowly convinced herself that she was in no danger of being found out. She began to relax as she got back in her car, cranked it, and drove away. She even found some levity in her made-up term about Sam's driver's license and patted herself on the back with a chuckle. "Points Elimination Register. Brilliant. Good thinking, Your Honor."

Marne Petakis slowly stood up from behind the bushes and turned off the video recording feature on her cell phone, squinting through the dust from Cassie's car as it picked up speed going down the dirt road.

"Got it."

She then dialed a number on her cell phone.

"Hello."

"Hey, it's me. I'm ready. Can you come get me?"

"Sure. On my way, Marne."

Jacob Hankins, the man who lived in the only house in sight of their meeting, an old man who hated the government at all its levels, had, unbeknownst to Sam and Cassie, watched their meeting and heard her shouting all the way to the back of his property where his henhouse is. He spat on the ground when he saw that it was Cassie Manson and was even more disgusted when he saw Marne Petakis emerge from the woods and clumsily step into the dirt road to await the arrival of her friend to give her a ride home.

"Damn Judge Manson," he said to himself. "Fined me for something I didn't do, didn't do at all. What the hell were you doing way out here? Go back to the city where you belong, bitch, you *and* that damn Marne Petakis."

Marne's friend from a few houses down the road from hers, Julia, arrived a couple of minutes later and stopped next to Marne. Marne opened the door and just before she stepped in she looked at Julie with that smug smile that she was so well-known for in this county and said in a voice loud enough for Jacob to hear, "I've got it on video. She's toast now!"

"What in the world?" said Jacob to no one in particular.

"SHERIFF'S OFFICE."

"Hello, this is Marne Petakis. Is Sheriff Portis in today?"

"No, ma'am, he's not usually in on Saturdays."

"Is it possible that you could reach him and ask him if he'd be willing to meet me today? I have some very important information about an investigation he's conducting and I want to get it to him right away."

"Actually, Ms. Petakis, he will be off for the next several days. He took a short vacation to see some out-of-town family for Thanksgiving since he doesn't like to be gone over holidays and wanted to be here during the Thanksgiving weekend. I can put you in touch with his chief deputy if you like."

"No, that's all right. I'll just meet with him when he returns. Thank you."

LATER THAT MORNING Jacob Hankins pulled into the local hardware store and went inside when he saw Rick Ambrose getting some sprinkler equipment. The two had been friends for years and Jacob even did some patio work for Rick at his house some time back.

"Jacob, long time. How've you been?"

"Pretty good, Rick. How about you?"

"Not too bad. So what brings you in here today?"

"Just gettin' some wheelbarrow parts."

"You still doing handyman work around the county?"

"Oh, yeah. Gotta make a livin' somehow. How's Louise?"

"Doing good. I'll tell her you asked about her."

"Say, Rick, y'all ain't got any more work for me at your place, have you? I'm still tryin' to pay off that damn fine I got for nothin'."

Rick laughed. "For nothing? Come on now, Jacob, they don't usually fine people for nothing. What did you do?"

"No, I mean it, Rick. I didn't do a damned thing. I got wrote up by that code enforcement lady for havin' a mess in my yard although it's been like that since back in the 60s when I first moved into that house. Why all of a sudden is it a problem where I store my old tools and stuff? They ain't hurtin' nobody where they are. And the way I've got it at least I know where everything is. If it was organized, I wouldn't be able to find a damned thing!"

Rick laughed. "I know the feeling. No, sorry, I think our place is in about as a good a shape as it's gonna be. But if we need you for something I'll be sure to let you know. That porch you finished looks really good." He turned to continue his shopping. "Well, good to see you, Jacob. My best to your wife. I hope you get that darn fine paid off soon. If I can put in a word for you at the courthouse let me know."

"Well, on that score, Rick, maybe you *could* help me out a little bit. I know your wife is good friends with that magistrate judge up there. She's the one who fined me. Anyway, I saw her earlier this mornin' meetin' with some guy. Seein' you reminded me that your wife is the clerk lady or somethin' up there, so maybe you could put in a good word for me, might buy me a little more time to pay it off. My wife does the cleanin' at the courthouse and she tried to talk to her about it, but that woman is about as easy to talk to as Godzilla."

"I'll see what I can do," chuckled Rick. "What do you mean, though, a meeting. Where?"

"On the dirt road out in front of my house. Strange lookin' situation, to tell ya the truth. They both parked their cars and got out, and he said somethin' she didn't like so she started railin' at him. She was mad as a wet settin' hen," he laughed. "I swear I thought she was gonna call the law and have him locked up right there on the spot. Anyway, he gave her some money and she drove off, kickin' up dirt all the way down the darn road. Couldn't even breathe for a spell out there."

"Gave her some money? You mean some guy gave money to Cassie Manson, right?"

"Yeah, that's her name. That judge up there. Don't know what it was all about, but he must've been behind in his fines or somethin'. And ya know the strangest part? Right after they both drove off that weirdo, Marne Petakis, come stumblin' out of the damn woods. Then she called some lady to come pick her up and before she got in her car she said, 'I got it on video!'. Damnedest thing I ever did see."

"Yeah, that is a little strange, isn't it? Well, it was good to see you, Jacob."

The two shook hands, said their good-byes and went their ways, but Jacob's comments left Rick wondering what Cassie was up to. He decided to stop by her house on the way back home. She came to the door wearing a bathrobe and with a blank expression on her face.

"Hey," he greeted.

"Hey, Rick. What brings you out this way?"

"I had something I wanted to ask you about. Were you out on Armour Road this morning?"

"Why do you ask?"

"Well, it's just that a friend of mine who lives out that way said he saw . . ."

He was interrupted by a man's voice coming from the back of the house.

"Who is it, Cassie?".

"I've got it, Aaron," she shouted and turned back to Rick.

"What the fuck?" said Rick.

"Now, Rick, you and I are just dating, so don't go all off about it. Besides, you're married yourself, and I don't complain when you crawl in bed with your damn wife every night, a wife you won't divorce, I might add."

Rick, now getting angry, stepped over the threshold of the front door, uninvited.

"Rick, don't start anything now. I think you'd better leave." She pointed to the outside.

But Rick was still miffed about her "cheating" on him, as he thought of it. He didn't mind being married and staying married long beyond the deadline Cassie had given him to get his divorce, but he was obviously one of those men who didn't want to share the woman he considered to be his own with anybody else. Then the man whose voice he heard stepped out into the living room and, as if to add insult to injury, he was wearing only his underwear. It was Aaron Ginn, the crooked real estate broker, a man easily thirty years her senior,

"Well, well, well, who have we here? If it ain't the crookedest damn businessman in the county."

"Rick, you'd better just do as Cassie says. This is her house, not yours. None of us needs any trouble."

"Well, my question still stands, Cassie. What were you doing out on Armour Road this morning? I heard a guy was giving you money. Why, what for? And what was that nosy Marne Petakis doing in the woods filming you?"

"Marne Petakis filming me? What the hell?"

Cassie became as pale as a ghost at hearing Rick's words, but she did have the presence of mind to refrain from saying about her embezzlement scheme.

"Yeah, he said that you were yelling at some guy about a fine or something, then he gave you some money, then you drove off, then Marne came out of the woods and somebody drove up to pick her up and she said something to him about having gotten something on video."

"Well, it's nothing that concerns you, Rick. It's none of your goddamn business, actually. How's that answer for you?"

Aaron laughed, infuriating Rick even more. He turned and stormed out of the house, the windows rattling as the door slammed.

"Oooh, that was interesting," said Aaron.

"It's not funny Aaron. Obviously that guy tipped off that goddamn Marne Petakis about me. You heard Rick say that she was in the woods filming me. Oh my God, Aaron. What if she's got me on video doing this shakedown? I could go to prison for this! I thought that you were the only other person who knew about this little scheme besides Angelina and Louise. I don't want anybody else being aware of anything, even Rick, and especially Marne." She sat down in a recliner and tilted her head back. "What the hell am I gonna do, Aaron?! This could be disastrous!"

"Oh, calm down, Cassie. I'm sure it's nothing. Besides, I told you from the get-go I've got you covered. I've been about as bulletproof as a human being can be when it comes to shady deals and I have way too much power in this town to let anything happen to you. I was one of your biggest supporters and I helped get you elected, and Louise too for that matter. So just don't fret it."

"I can't help but fret about it, Aaron. I've got to nip this thing in the bud, and right now. What if the wrong people found out about it? I tell you, I just feel like I'm playing with fire and I sure don't want to get burnt."

"Well, you *are* fucking another woman's husband, Cassie, so you're playing with fire to begin with."

Cassie's eyes began to well up with worry and dread, as well as anger at Aaron for his remark. She could see her whole career and life unraveling at the thought of losing control of this situation, long before it even happened.

Then she swallowed hard, took a deep breath and sat up straight in her chair. She would do whatever she had to do to keep the status quo, no matter what it took. No matter what.

Then her narcissism and hubris overtook her fear. She stood up, took off her bathrobe, slapped Aaron, went down on her knees, pulled down his underwear, grabbed his dick and started stroking it. She opened her mouth and deep-throated him to the sound of his groaning.

"Now that's my girl."

She took her mouth away long enough to say, "Fuck you. No, better idea . . . fuck me." And the two headed back into the bedroom.

Panic Sets In

When Rick got home from Cassie's house he busied himself in his shop with various little tasks he had been wanting to do, and some he hadn't been. Although he couldn't let Louise know how he felt, he could barely suppress his anger and frustration at Cassie, sneaking an old man into her bed while he wasn't looking. He was building a porch swing, something he had been working on for some time, and every nail he drove got an extra strong pounding with each strike. Louise came out to his shop to tell him that lunch was ready. He answered her without turning to face her.

"OK, I'll be in there in a minute."

"Well, that was terse. You're welcome."

Rick laid down his hammer and turned around to face her. "I'm sorry. I appreciate lunch. I'm just a little distracted today, that's all."

"Everything OK?"

"Yeah, everything's fine. Just a lot of stuff to do."

The two went inside just as the children were finishing up their meal. They took a seat at the empty table and started eating, Rick never looking up from his sandwich and potato chips. Louise stared at him for a few seconds.

"Rick, you've been acting awfully strange lately. Is there something you're not telling me?

"No, no, Louise. There's nothing. I just want to do a really good job next week for this next customer I've got. He's a pretty wealthy guy and I want to have his business for the long term. I've got that on my mind, that's all."

"You sure that's all?"

"Yeah, that's it. I just want things to go well at work."

Still not satisfied with his answer but unwilling to pursue the matter any further, Louise finished her meal, took up the plates and left the table.

They whole family sat in the living room that evening after supper. Rick continued to stew in the thoughts of Cassie with Aaron Ginn. He fantasized about a way to pay her back for screwing Aaron when he thought *he* was her man. Finally, he snapped his fingers and looked to Louise.

"Hey, why don't you see if your mom and dad would like to have the kids over to spend the night tonight? You and me need us a little alone time."

The kids heard him and started jumping up and down. They were always only too willing to visit their grandparents who were always so good to them. Louise gave Rick that sinister smile and a wink that told him that she was just as interested in a night alone as he was. She called her mother and an hour later the kids were on their way to a night of lax discipline, chocolate chip cookies and watching tv with no bedtime.

THAT NIGHT CASSIE FOUND herself very anxious to talk to Louise about Marne filming her taking a payment from a defendant. Ever since Aaron had left that evening she had kept it to herself, but real panic was beginning to set in.

Finally, sat around eight o'clock she decided to call. When the phone rang Louise lazily reached for it on the nightstand beside her bed intending to push the button that declines the call, but being so tipsy from all the wine she had drunk she accidentally hit the wrong spot on the screen and answered it. Thinking that the call had gone unanswered, she turned her attention back to her husband. Rick, also feeling high from the generous amount of wine he had consumed, buried his head between her breasts. Neither of them knew that Cassie was on the other end of the phone repeatedly saying, "Hello? Hello?" They couldn't hear her, but what they didn't realize was that she could hear them.

"Good," slurred Rick. "No calls tonight. I have plans for your ass. Come on, let's get started. We don't have all that many nights when the kids aren't here."

Louise laughed.

"I know, Rick. Put that big dick down there where it can do some good. No, on second thought stick it in my face. My mouth is watering."

Rick and Louise began their bedroom fun without concern about the noise they made, oblivious to Cassie's listening ears on the other end of Louise's phone still sitting on the nightstand. She heard them moan and groan, heard Rick scream with delight as Louise slurped while she sucked him, heard her coo with ecstasy as Rick licked her, starting with her left foot, slowly making his way to her right foot while stopping for some time in between, then working his way back to her left foot, and back and forth, back and forth, with Louise moaning louder and louder each time he licked her hungry love canal.

"Okay, Rick, *now* you can put it where it can do some good. I'm ready. I'm *really* ready."

Rick entered her and his dick slid in and out, first slowly, then faster, then as fast as he could. They changed positions several times, each time producing more pleasure than the time before. After half an hour they exploded together in a thundering orgasm for them both.

"Oh, goddamn, Louise, that was good. That's the best pussy I've had in months."

Cassie grew angrier and angrier as she listened to them, especially his last comment. "The best pussy I've had in months?" Really? Their night of lovemaking was more passionate than she had ever had with Rick, and it infuriated her to no end.

When the sounds finally quieted down and she knew that they had finished their night of ecstasy Cassie disconnected the call and went to her bedroom. She sat on the bed for a few minutes and thought about how she wished she had Rick with her at that moment so she could squeeze his balls until they popped like little balloons.

That son of a bitch. That goddamn son of a bitch. How could he do this to her? And the best pussy he had had in months? What the fuck? Oh, how she wanted to cut off his dick with a rusty knife and shove it down his throat. Or up his ass.

She stewed in her morbid thoughts for a while and caught herself running her fingers between her legs, which were curiously wet. She laid on the bed, put on a porn movie, and thought about Rick while she masturbated herself to sleep.

THE NEXT MORNING CASSIE meandered over to the coffee pot and poured herself a big cup, bigger than she usually had, taking it black this time. Then the worry over the Marne thing again began to simmer in her mind. And simmer. And simmer some more. By the end of the weekend she was a nervous wreck.

But Rick. Oh, Rick, now that's another story. He had done the unthinkable in her mind, fucked his own wife. Never mind that she was seeing Aaron Ginn. No, Rick had betrayed her, that's how she saw it, just as Rick perceived her seeing Ginn as betraying him.

A match made in hell.

MONDAY MORNING SAW a busy courthouse with it being the week of Thanksgiving. People who had lawsuits to file and wanted to get them off their minds before the holiday were scampering in and out of the clerk's office. Royceland Kane, the attorney who had won the Blakely murder trial was busy searching titles in the deed room, tying up the last loose ends of the real estate closings he wanted to clear out before Thursday. Cassie brazenly walked into Louise's office in her usual fashion, her air of authority permeating throughout the office as if to say, "You lowly deputy clerks are nothing compared to me." She strutted in, sat down in a flaunting manner and leaned back in the chair facing Louise.

"Good morning," greeted Louise.

"What's good about it?"

"What do you mean?"

"Louise, we need to have a talk. Something's happened."

"Shut the door."

Cassie stood, shut the office door and sat back down. "Over the weekend I met a guy to collect some fine money. It turns out he cuts the grass for Marne Petakis. A friend of mine said that he saw a man at the hardware store who lives out there near where I met the guy and he saw the whole thing, saw me talk to the defendant, saw me collect the money from him, everything."

"Oooh, that's not good, Cassie."

"Oh, that isn't even the worst part. The man said he then saw Marne Petakis come out of the woods and call somebody to come pick her up. When she got in the car she said something about having a video of me. Louise, I'm scared shitless."

"Damn, Cassie. That can't get to the authorities. If Marne gets that video to the sheriff, you're screwed. Hell, we're all screwed. What if they start looking into the county records and see that Angelina and me are also doing this same type of shit?"

"How do we know she hasn't already gotten it to the sheriff?"

"He's out of town until tomorrow night. That gives us today and most of the day tomorrow. We've got to get our hands on that video, Cassie. We've got to."

"How?"

"I don't know. Let me think about a plan. Just let me think for a little while. I'll give you a call. In the meantime you'd better go across the hall and tell Angelina. Her ass is in this too."

Cassie left Louise's office without another word. It'd better be a damn good plan, she thought. She went to the state court office and met with Angelina. She told her of the horrific events of the past weekend.

"What?! You've been videotaped doing one of your collections?! Cassie, that's terrible. That damn Marne Petakis could ruin us all. If she starts nosing around the county records it could expose all three of us."

"I know, Angelina. That's what Louise says too. What do we do?"

"I don't know, but you'd damn well better figure out something. You've got your court, I've got mine and Louise has her office over there. I know we're all doing this but we're doing our own things in our own offices. I don't want anybody else going down because of your fuckup."

Cassie could hardly believe Angelina's sudden burst of what she perceived as hostility and selfishness.

"Look, y'all got into doing this shit voluntarily, Angelina. I never twisted anybody's arm. I just told you two about it and y'all ran with it. Now, we've got to stick together and figure out a way through this."

"Cassie, I'm not going to prison for you or anybody else. Now, you'd better come up with a viable plan to get that video from that goddamn Marne Petakis as soon as you can before the sheriff gets back. That's assuming that she hasn't already shared it with somebody else."

CASSIE LEFT THE OFFICE shortly after lunch and went home, her nerves way too wracked to keep her mind on working. She was surprised to see Louise pull into her driveway a few minutes later. Cassie met her in the driveway.

"Tell me that you've got an idea, Louise. I'm about to go crazy here."

"Is anybody else here?"

"No. There never is."

"Let's go inside."

The two women went into Cassie's living room and sat down. Louise took a long look at the floor and slowly raised her eyes to meet Cassie's.

"Cassie, I never, ever thought I'd hear myself utter these words, but these are drastic times and you know what they say about drastic times."

"Yeah."

"There was a murder trial a little earlier this year, remember? The guy was acquitted, but I think anybody with a brain knew he killed the lady. His name was Harry Blakely. Royce got him off but like I said, I think he's a killer who just simply dodged a bullet."

"OK. What about him?"

"Cassie, if he can commit one murder and get away with it, then maybe he can do it again."

Cassie gasped as she began to understand Louise's meaning. Louise could see Cassie's surprise and tried to justify herself.

"We've got to keep this video from getting to the sheriff or any other authorities. If she hasn't already sent it to anybody then we've still got a chance."

"You want us to get him to kill Marne?"

"I don't like that any more than you do, Cassie, but if he can do it and is willing to, then we've got to consider all our options. And right now, this is the only one I've managed to come up with."

Cassie couldn't believe what she was hearing. Have somebody murdered? Are they that type of people? Are they that desperate? Could they actually do such a thing?

But money has a very strong allure, and these three embezzlers wanted to keep what they had taken from the county. But even could be the least of their worries; the prospect of being prosecuted for their crimes and actually going to prison was something none of the three could bear. Cassie finally resolved herself to at least consider the proposal.

"Are you game?"

Cassie hesitated, scowled, grabbed a tissue to wipe her forehead, and said, "Yes. I'm in. Where does he live?"

CASSIE DROVE UP TO the old, dilapidated house on one of the few streets in Shady Dale, a small town on the northern end of Jasper County. But this house boasted no clapboard walls that didn't need repair and painting, no roof that didn't leak, and no porch that had a single fresh plank on it nor a screen that would keep out a fly with a hangover. She timidly walked up to the front door, careful as she stepped to avoid winding up on the ground underneath, and lightly knocked on the door. A man in his 40s, short and stout with messy grey hair that looked like it hadn't been washed in weeks, an unkempt beard and mustache that looked like it hadn't been trimmed in as long, shorts with no shirt and a pot belly hanging over the waistband opened the door with a beer can in his hand. His appearance was a far cry from how he had looked during his trial when Royceland Kane had instructed him to dress like he was "going to your grandmama's church on Sunday."

"Can I help you?" he asked.

"Yes, sir. Mr. Blakely?"

"That's me."

"I'm Cassie Manson. I work at the courthouse. How're you today?"

"I'm OK. What do you need?"

This man, though cordial, obviously wasn't in the mood for conversation, especially with someone from the courthouse, a place he had gotten his fill of during his trial.

"I was wondering if I could talk to you for a minute or two."

"About what?"

"Well, I have a, uh, business proposition for you, Mr. Blakely."

Mr. Blakely hesitated for a minute, looked Cassie up and down in a leering manner that made her feel strangely uncomfortable and finally said, "OK. Come on in."

He opened the broken screen door, swatting to keep as many flies as possible from swarming in on this warmer-than-normal late November day as Cassie walked inside. His efforts were unsuccessful.

"You want a glass of tea or something?"

"Uh, no, thank you. I just wanted to talk to you about something that's come up with me and some friends of mine."

"Uh, OK. What's on your mind?"

"Mr. Blakely, I understand that you were tried for murder a while back down at the courthouse in Monticello."

"Well, the jury found me not guilty, Miss Manson. My lawyer says that they can't try me again for that murder. He says it'd be double jeopardy. So if you're here trying to get a confession or something, you can forget it."

"Oh, no, Mr. Blakely," said Cassie with a chuckle. "That's not at all why I'm here." She looked around the living room and craned her neck to look down the hallway. "Tell me, Mr. Blakely, are we alone here?"

"Yes, ma'am. Ain't a God's soul here but us. You can talk plain."

"Good. Mr. Blakely, what I'm going to say cannot be repeated to another person. I want us to be clear on that before I begin. Are we clear on that point, sir?"

Mr. Blakely took another swig from his beer can. "You betcha."

"I'm of the opinion that your verdict might not have been, well, how can I say this? Accurate?"

"What do you mean?"

Cassie again looked around, although she felt sure by now that they were alone in the house.

"I mean that I think you did it. I think you committed the murder and simply got away with it. I'm sorry if that's a little too plainspoken, Mr. Blakely."

"Well, what if I did? The damn jury already said I didn't do it, Miss Manson. Y'all can't try me again, you know that."

"Yes, I know you can't be tried again for the same crime, Mr. Blakely. But again, that's not what I'm here about."

"So just exactly what are you here about then?"

She sat back in her chair and decided to change the tone of the conversation.

"You know, I think I will have a glass of that ice tea, Mr. Blakely, if you don't mind, sir."

"What? Oh, OK. I'll pour you one. Let me wash out a glass."

Mr. Blakely returned a couple of minutes later with a tall glass of sweet ice tea for Cassie, and she found the glass surprisingly clean and the tea equally good and refreshing.

"Thank you, sir. Now, if we can be plain with each other, I want you to consider something. It's obvious that you don't have a lot of money, Mr. Blakely. I mean, that jalopy you drive out there in the yard looks like it's on its last leg, this entire house looks like it's about to fall in, and I think your front porch was built before before man landed on the moon."

Mr. Blakely began to laugh at Cassie's reference to the moon landing, but it was obvious there was something about the time reference that was beyond him.

"That was over fifty years ago, Mr. Blakely. But let me get to the point. You've shown that you can commit a murder and get away with it. I have somebody I would like to have killed and you came to mind as the man for the job."

Mr. Blakely stared at her for a minute and laid down his beer. He picked it back up and stared at her for a few more seconds.

"Is this some kind of a set-up, Miss Manson? Are you trying to get me back in trouble with the law again?!"

"No, Mr. Blakely, I promise you I'm not. It's just that I've found myself in a situation that needs your skills, that's all. And frankly, that murder you committed and got away with was very impressive, to say the least. Now I'm asking if you're willing to commit one for hire."

Mr. Blakely shook his head back and forth as if trying to figure out the most unsolvable math problem every conceived. He again laid down his beer can and looked Cassie straight in the eye.

"What did you have in mind?"

"Well, how much would you charge?"

"Depends on the target. Who is he?"

"It's a woman in Jasper County. Her name is Marne Petakis."

"Marne Petakis. Seems like I've heard of her. Ain't she the one that's always stirring up shit with people, especially courthouse people?"

"That's the one."

"Don't know much about her other than that. Where does she live and work?"

"Well, she works from her house on a dirt road way out in the county, about five miles outside the city. So she's there most of the time, when she's not out stirring up trouble for everybody else."

"Does she live with family?"

"I don't think so."

"Well, I might be interested for twenty thousand dollars, Miss Manson."

"Twenty thousand dollars. OK. I'll be in touch, but there's a catch – this has to be done very quickly. Like tonight or tomorrow morning. Is that understood, Mr. Blakely?"

"Well, then, I'd better add a 'convenience fee' of five thousand more. Make it twenty five thousand and you've got a deal. Guaranteed results, Miss Manson."

"Very good, Mr. Blakely," said Cassie as she stood and walked towards the broken front door. "I'll get back to you in a couple of hours."

Mr. Blakely stood to walk Cassie to the door like a proper gentleman, which again surprised her, then even opened the door for her as she stepped back out onto the rickety porch. As she reached the steps she turned to Mr. Blakely for the last time.

"One thing I want to make clear, Mr. Blakely. No matter what, my name never gets mentioned to anyone. You're on your own with this, even if you get caught, you're on your own. Do we understand each other? And it has to be done by no later than noon tomorrow. After that, there's no deal and you'll have to pay the money back. If I can come up with the money where do you want me to bring it?"

Without a word Mr. Blakely pointed over his shoulder to the house they both just came out of.

"OK, then. You can look for me later today, Mr. Blakely. And remember, if you mention my name to anyone you'll wind up like Marne Petakis. Understood?"

Mr. Blakely's answer was a loud burp as he crushed the empty beer can and tossed it in the yard.

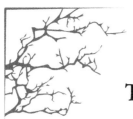

The Murder

Cassie's lack of appetite caused by her nervousness made her stomach growl again as the afternoon autumn sun began to recede in the sky, making the shadows longer and longer each day while the wind cooled down the middle Georgia November heat. The forecast called for rain that night and into the morning with a cold front coming in afterwards and pushing out the clouds, promising much colder temperatures for the rest of the week and on into the Thanksgiving holiday. She slowly drove into Mr. Blakely's yard and parked her car. This time he greeted her as she got out and walked towards the porch with the bundle of cash in her hand that she had taken from her "cash stash". But it had really bugged her that neither Louise nor Angelina had been willing to pitch in their fair share. That twenty-five thousand dollar "withdrawal" had really put a dent in her stash.

"So you're back, Miss Manson. You got somethin' for me?"

"Let's go inside."

The two sat down in the living room, Mr. Blakely in a chair and Cassie on the couch. The dust from the cushions floated in the air as their ample asses hit the fabric, creating an eerie atmosphere in the late afternoon sunlight coming in through the curtainless windows.

"It's all there, Mr. Blakely. Twenty-five thousand. You can count it."

"I intend to," he replied as he took the bundle of cash from Cassie. He sat back and counted it bill by bill. When he had finished he smiled and looked up at her.

"Yep, it's twenty-five thousand, all right. I know where she lives and what she looks like. A picture of her would help, though."

"I don't have a picture of her, but she's an ugly little woman with long, curly black hair and glasses that sit on the end of her nose for looking down on everybody else."

"Got it."

"'Got it' is fine, Mr. Blakely, but time is running out. You need to get busy tonight, and I mean right now. If she lives until she gets a chance to meet with the sheriff about a particular matter that means a lot to me and some other people, the deal's off. And in that case I want every goddamn bit of that money back. And I won't stop until I get it. Do you understand that, Mr. Blakely?"

"Wow, you're a little tiger, Miss Manson. But don't you worry your pretty little head about a thing. I'll get my good ole .30-.30 rifle and have her sleeping with the worms by tomorrow morning."

"See that you do, Mr. Blakely. Now get to work. And remember, you're on your own."

CASSIE WENT BACK TO her house and got out her cell phone. She called Rick. Yes, fuck it, she said to herself. I'm going to call him from my cell phone to his cell phone. Screw Louise. She didn't pitch in a goddamn penny to help pay for Blakely. Besides, she had a plan. She would get Rick to come to her house while Blakely was out doing his job. That way she would have an alibi should the sheriff ever somehow connect her to Marne's murder.

Yes, that's the plan. A brilliant plan. She dialed his number.

"Hello."

"Hey, it's me. You busy tonight?"

"Oh, hey, Matt. Something wrong at one of the job sites?" Rick lowered his head to better muffle the sound of Cassie's voice coming over his cell phone and ducked into his shop outside.

"What the fuck are you doing calling me like this, Cassie? You know better than to call my number! If Louise ever looks at my phone she'll see that you called. What's the matter with you?"

"I need for you to come over here tonight, Rick. Screw discretion. I've got something for you, and it ain't pumpkin pie."

"Cassie, you know I can't do that. I'm at the house with Louise and the kids. What in the world would I come up with for an excuse?"

"You could tell her that a sprinkler has busted or something. She thinks you're talking to Matt from work anyway, right? Anyway, just think of something, Rick. I mean it."

Puzzled, Rick hung up the phone and walked back inside the house. He saw Louise putting away the dishes out of the dishwasher.

"I've got some bad news, Louise. Matt just called and it seems that a sprinkler system we put in today just broke and water is spewing all over the place at a guy's house. I'm going to have to go tend to it."

"Aw, Rick, really? I had planned on us doing some of our Thanksgiving dinner cooking tonight. Do you really have to go?"

"I'm afraid so, honey."

Rick kissed Louise good-bye and left in his work truck, wasting no time in getting out of the driveway and out of sight.

HARRY BLAKELY WENT to his closet, got out his Marlin .30-.30 rifle, loaded it and walked to his car.

"This is gonna be an easy twenty-five thousand dollars."

He arrived at Marne Petakis' house around eight o'clock and pulled over onto the side of the road directly across from her house, a nice brick home in a very secluded area on a paved road that constantly needed repair. The effects of his day-long beer drinking were finally beginning to subside and his mind was becoming clearer and clearer, sharper and sharper. He crouched down behind his car with his rifle in his hand and watched and waited. And waited. And waited.

Finally a car pulled into her driveway at around 10:00. It was Marne. She got out, shut her door and began walking toward the front door of her house. Blakely felt the adrenaline surge in his body as he aimed his rifle at her head. He closed one eye and trained the other one through the sights of his rifle. He pulled back the hammer and heard it click, sounding much louder to him than it really was. He turned his head from side to side one last time to make sure that no cars were coming, then repositioned his line of sight. The coast was clear. He aimed his rifle and just when he was about to pull the trigger she dropped something and bent down to pick it up.

Blakely mumbled to himself, "Son of a bitch."

She picked up the paper she had dropped, snapped her fingers, turned around towards the road and said out loud "the mail."

Blakely squatted lower to the ground to cover himself behind his car, hoping she wouldn't notice it parked there. Marne briskly walked to her mailbox, oblivious to the danger to her life that waited just across the road. She got closer and closer to the end of the driveway, reached for the mailbox, began to open it, and a loud shot rang out.

Marne was dead.

BLAKELY SAT DOWN IN his living room and opened himself yet another beer to celebrate his success. He had made some money, a goodly amount of it, more money that he had seen for a very long time and for only a few minutes' work. Having killed before he felt no remorse, no regrets, no sympathy for his victim. And unlike his last murder he felt totally insulated on this one. The bullet had struck Marne at such an angle that it went through her head and into the woods far behind her house so it was unrecoverable. He had split her head open very neatly with one shot, the kill shot, just like dropping a deer with a well-placed bullet. Whatever this woman had done, he reasoned, justified her death. If that Miss Manson wanted her dead so badly that she was willing to pay this kind of money to have her killed then yes, Marne must've done something to deserve it. Such was the logic of a cold, feelingless hit man.

Meanwhile, on the other side of the county sirens blared through the cool November night air bringing deputies to Marne's country home. The ambulance was already there when the fleet of deputies arrived, having been called by a passing neighbor on his way home from the church Thanksgiving program who had looked with horror as he saw Marne's lifeless body in the headlights of his pickup truck.

The ambulance attendants stood around the lifeless body of Marne Petakis while the sheriff's department investigators took photographs, made measurements, calculated various angles of shots and so forth, and in general conducted their preliminary crime scene investigation. After a while the deputies gave the attendants the go-ahead to remove the body and they did the best they could to put her on the stretcher and load her into the big waiting double doors of the ambulance without spilling her brains all over the concrete driveway. Even though she was obviously dead, they did not have the legal authority to pronounce her so, so they whisked her away accompanied by lights and sirens to the local hospital in town. But they knew she was dead. Very dead. Her skull was split in two. One of her eyeballs was missing. Her tongue had been bitten off from the snapping together of her teeth at the jolt of lightning that passed through her head. Yes, she was dead.

Captain Markham, the chief deputy of the Sheriff's Department, raced to the scene to find five deputies, two of whom were vomiting behind one of the big pine trees in Marne's neatly-manicured lawn. He frowned at them and gathered the other deputies for a briefing.

"Well, Captain, I was the first one here and the ambulance attendants were waiting for our go-ahead to put her on the stretcher when I arrived. She was lying on the ground and she was a mess. Looks like a head shot. The attendants did what they're supposed to do, but she's dead. No doubt about that."

"What about the witness who called it in?"

"Some guy who lives down the road a ways. Said he'd been to the Thanksgiving service at the church in town and was on his way home. He drove past here about 10:30 and saw the body in the front yard near the road. I interviewed him when I got here and he said that he never saw anyone else, not even any passing cars. Whoever did this was quick in doing it and didn't waste any time getting out of here either."

"The church service is usually over around eight thirty. Wonder why he was so late coming home?"

"Don't know, Captain."

"Any ideas about the origin of the shot?"

"From the blood splatter I'd say it came from over there," he said, pointing across the road towards the spot where Blakely had been. "No shell casings, though. No debris that I could find, but I plan to check again tomorrow after daybreak."

"Well," said the captain, "if it came from across the road then the bullet is probably long gone. But check the side of the house anyway just in case it might have landed there. Maybe it ricocheted or something, or his angle was more in line with the house than we're thinking. Maybe we'll get lucky. And check over there for tracks too. Maybe we'll find something there. But do it quick; it looks like it's about to rain."

The deputies continued to put the crime scene ribbon all around the area well into the night and past the first break of morning. They looked and looked, metal detectors and magnifying glasses in hand, hoping to find a clue. But they found nothing.

In the early afternoon Sheriff Portis arrived, having left his vacation earlier than planned when he was told about the murder. Murder in this county was a rare event and he wanted to be sure that he gave it his full attention. He went directly to the crime scene after going home first to change into his uniform. He found the Captain still there directing the investigation.

"You mean there's nothing, Captain? No casings, no trash left by the shooter, no tire tracks, nothing?"

"Not a thing, Sheriff."

"Who was notified as next of kin?"

"That would be her son, Randy. I called him early this morning. He's pretty tore up, as you can imagine. And right here at the holidays too."

"I know she doesn't have much in the way of neighbors way out here, but I want the few that are nearby canvassed and interviewed. Maybe somebody heard a shot or something."

The captain went about a quarter of a mile down the road and pulled into a driveway to visit who was the closest thing Marne had to a neighbor. He knocked on the door and an old woman in her 80s answered.

"Can I help you, officer?"

"Yes, ma'am. I'm Captain Markham of the Sheriff's Department. We're investigating the shooting from last night."

"Shooting?"

"Yes, ma'am. Ms. Petakis was shot and I'm afraid she didn't make it. I was wondering if you remembered hearing or seeing anything or anybody that might help us."

"Ms. Petakis, Marne? She was shot? She's dead?"

"Yes, ma'am, I'm afraid so. Did you happen to see or hear anything unusual last night, any gunshots or anything?"

"As a matter of fact I did hear a gunshot, but I just figured it was one of those idiots shooting at a deer. Hunters are all around here this time of year, you know. They disturb me a lot. But that's all I heard."

"Do you know about what time that was?"

"Oh, I guess a little after 10:00. I was about to head to bed, so yes, it must've been around that time."

"Did you see any cars or trucks going down the road at around that time?"

"No, sir, I can't say that I did."

"You don't have a security camera or anything like that by chance, do you?"

"I'm afraid not, Captain. I'm sorry. I guess I'm not much help."

"Oh, I appreciate your help a lot, ma'am. If you think of anything else would you please call me?" he said as he handed her his business card.

"I sure will."

The captain returned to the crime scene and reported his conversation with the lady to the sheriff.

"Not much to go on right now I guess, eh, sheriff?"

"Not really. We could make a list of people who were her enemies, but I don't suppose we can call everybody in the county, can we?"

Captain Edwards laughed, as much to break the somber mood at such a scene as in response to the sheriff's joke, and walked towards the house to examine the exterior for bullet holes.

THE NEXT DAY, WEDNESDAY, the day before Thanksgiving, was a holiday for the courthouse. Cassie kept a constant eye on Facebook for information about the murder, a subject that filled the screen with comments from the locals. There was precious little detail in their posts, but it was clear that Marne Petakis had been murdered. She smiled at each entry she read, knowing that the threat to her and her lucrative little scheme was safe and sound.

Then she remembered – she had forgotten to tell Harry Blakely to get Marne's cell phone!

Panic began to set in again in her mind. What if her cell phone was collected by the sheriff's deputies and they went through it? She had presumed all along that Marne had recorded the meeting on her cell phone. After all, she reasoned, nobody has video cameras any more, not now that everybody has cell phones. But then again, what if she *didn't* use her phone? Maybe she did have a video camera and it's not being confiscated and examined. But what if she didn't? Oh my God, she thought! If they go through that and see me taking money from that damn guy I've had it!

The mind of the inexperienced criminal. They always make a mistake. She called Louise.

"Hello."

"It's me. You've heard?"

"Oh, yes, it's all over the county."

"Can you come over?"

"Today? Tomorrow's Thanksgiving, Cassie. I'm cooking today."

"Please!"

"OK, OK. Just calm down. And don't say anything else on the phone. I'm on my way."

Louise arrived to find Cassie sitting at the kitchen table. Her eyes were bloodshot, her hair was a mess, and she looked like she hadn't slept in weeks.

"What's the matter? It looks like Blakely pulled it off. We're clean, Cassie. Just relax."

"Louise, I forgot to tell him to get her cell phone. What if the sheriff gets it and goes through it? He'll see the whole goddamned thing."

Louise looked towards the ceiling.

"Oh, Cassie, I thought for sure you would have told him to get her phone! Well, maybe she didn't use her phone to record it."

"I thought about that, but I'll bet she did. Everybody uses their phones as cameras these days. Nobody carries a damn video camera around unless they're making a goddamn movie!"

"Can you get a hold of the camera? I mean, you go to the sheriff's department all the time doing magistrate stuff. Maybe you can mosey your way to the evidence room and get your hands on it."

"Louise, do you realize what all that would involve? And they have video cameras in the sheriff's department too, and they're all over the place. I hate to think of what would happen to me if I got caught taking evidence in a case with an active investigation."

"Well, what do you think will happen to you if they see the footage?"

"Oh, God, what have I gotten myself into?"

Thanksgiving

Thanksgiving morning started very early at the houses of both Angelina Black and Louise Ambrose. The turkeys were stuffed and placed in the ovens around 5:00 A.M. with the basting brushes lying on the kitchen counters in their bowls of butter. Both women had managed to put to rest the worry that Cassie had failed to rid herself of, at least for today.

Cassie's house boasted no turkey in the oven. The events of the past few days had literally destroyed her holiday cheer and having a nice, relaxing Thanksgiving dinner was the last thing on her evil little mind. All she could think about was getting her hands on that video.

But presumably, Sheriff Portis now had possession of the all-important cell phone of the late Marne Petakis. How in the world could Cassie possibly get her hands on it? What could she do?

As she sat at the dining room table sipping her morning coffee and gently gnawing on the ceramic cup she decided to go to the sheriff's department and at least try to retrieve it from the evidence room. After all, what was one more crime now? She was already involved in a murder and embezzlement.

She pulled up at the sheriff's department and walked to the window where the holiday crew was.

"Oh, hello, Judge," said the officer on duty. "What brings you here on Thanksgiving Day?"

"I just wanted to see if I left something in the back the other day when I was out here doing some bond hearings. I think I might have left my favorite ink pen. I know that seems trivial, but it was a Christmas gift from my dad before he died. Can you buzz me in the door so I can go take a look?"

"Sure," replied the officer did as she hit the button that opened the door to the back of the building. Cassie went to the room where she does bond hearings, an informal little room but one that had been arranged in such a way as to bear a faint resemblance to a courtroom. She was relieved when she saw no one else in that part of the building, all of the deputies either out on patrol or off for the holiday.

She casually walked back to the courtroom and pretended to be looking for her pen. After a few minutes she walked back out into the hallway and headed for the exit. But then she looked all around once more to make sure that the area was clear and took a few extra steps toward the evidence room, which was often curiously kept unlocked. "Oh, please God, let it be unlocked today," she said to herself.

Her hand shook as she reached for the doorknob. She nervously wrapped her fingers around it and turned it.

The door opened.

She breathed a sigh of relief and hurriedly stepped inside, hoping and praying that no one had noticed her on the monitors. She quickly scanned the shelves looking for Marne Petakis' name. Sure enough, she saw a cubbyhole marked "Petakis – Murder".

Her hands grabbed the stack of papers from the shelf and she began going through them as fast as she could. There were papers, files, photographs, a driver's license, the blood-soaked envelopes from the mailbox that was splattered when she got shot . . . but no cell phone.

"Oh my God, the sheriff's got it!"

She put the items back in the slot from which she had removed them and dejectedly left the room, returning to the command center.

"Did you find it, Judge?" asked the officer who had let her in.

"Find what? Oh, my pen. Yes, I did. Thank you."

"You're welcome," answered the officer, surprised that Cassie didn't remember that she had come in specifically to look for her lost ink pen. The officer buzzed the door and the judge left.

"All I can do now is hope that the sheriff doesn't look at the video."

AFTER THANKSGIVING dinner Sheriff Portis sat down in his favorite recliner and turned on the football game. The Detroit Lions. Always the Detroit Lions on Thanksgiving.

He finished his slice of pumpkin pie and laid down the saucer and fork when his eye caught a cell phone sitting on the coffee table. Funny, he didn't remember getting a new phone. Then he remembered that he had brought it home from the office the day before and laid it down on the table to charge it up. He picked it up and saw the taped-on marker on the back that said "Petakis".

He turned it on and to his surprise, it needed no passcode. "That makes it easier," he thought. "No need to get an expert to get me in it." He looked at the screen and saw a photo of Marne and her dog.

"Likely the only real friend she had in the world." Sheriff Portis felt a little ashamed for thinking that way about a dead woman, but it was probably true. Marne got along with almost no one.

The sheriff went from screen to screen, seeing nothing that he felt would be of any relevance to his murder investigation. He decided to go through her text messages and saw text after text filled with venom and vitriol about this person and that person, this county employee and that county employee, this elected official and that elected official. In fact, there were so many that he got tired of reading them. Besides, nothing in any of them gave the sheriff any indication that someone was conspiring to have her murdered. Silenced, yes, but not murdered. He eventually cut the phone off, put it down and turned his attention back to the game. He made a mental note to give the phone to Justin, Marne's son, when he got back to the office after Thanksgiving.

But the events of the week would not recede from his mind on this holiday afternoon. First he had the allegations by Marne that the two judges were somehow not collecting the fines they should be collecting, especially in light of the increase in cases coming before them. The word "embezzlement" crossed his mind more than once. Then she winds up murdered with no clues and a county full of people who hated her. Sheriff Portis had a lot to think about on this Thanksgiving day.

Maybe it was time to give Judge Manson another visit. And this time visit Judge Black as well.

CASSIE'S THANKSGIVING dinnertime passed without so much as a processed turkey sandwich. She ate bologna for lunch, then had a milkshake and some olives. Her mind raced with the thoughts of what she had done and what would happen to her should her criminal enterprises be found out. And the worry over Marne's cell phone and the video it possibly contained had caused her to reach for the all-important tissues again. As long as the sheriff didn't see it, or if it wasn't on there at all, she was all right. But what if Marne did record it on her phone and it was discovered? She began to think of the next step in making something happen that would protect her from any suspicions.

She arrived at the courthouse office the next Monday morning with a haggard look on her face, sleepless for the past few nights, no rest for the weary. She had even noticed a few pounds dropped from her ample frame. She had spent more time in the bathroom than she had ever spent before.

Yes, Judge Cassie Manson was worried. Very worried.

There had to be a way to bring this consternation to an end. She thought and thought and thought. How can I make this whole thing go away? How can I make the murder investigation end with a suspect who can be convicted and thereby keep me from any suspicion while at the same time diverting attention away from my embezzlement?

Telling the authorities about Harry Blakely was out of the question. After all, she was the one who had hired him, who had visited him at his home in Shady Dale, who had paid him the money that she had foolishly touched with her own hands, leaving her fingerprints all over the bills. No, that would never do.

She had to figure out a way to give the authorities another suspect, someone new, someone they could pin this whole thing on and actually get a conviction in court for the crime of murder. But who? Think, she said to herself, think!

Maybe one of these grifters set to appear in her court that she had swindled. No, none of them would be viable candidates. She would have to know where they were at the time of the murder so they couldn't give the sheriff a good alibi.

Maybe somebody she had issued an arrest warrant for. No, they wouldn't really work either. Again, she would have to know what they were doing that night and at that time, or else they could have an alibi as well.

Then the light bulb lit up.

Rick.

Oh yes, that damn Rick. He had been having an affair with her for a while, his wife didn't know about it, a wife he seemed to be unwilling to divorce, and he got all bent out of shape when he saw her with Denny, acting like he owned her. And he was the perfect patsy. He was with her at the time of the murder, so what was he going to say to the sheriff? "I couldn't have committed the murder, Sheriff, I was fucking the magistrate judge when it happened." Cassie felt like a genius when she thought about how she had prompted him to come to her house so as to give *her* the perfect alibi, and now she had evolved that idea into blaming him for the murder. Who better for a viable suspect in a murder case to divert the sheriff's attention away from her? Brilliant!

Yes, Rick was the perfect one to pin this one. But she had to involve Louise. If she could get Louise to turn against him then between the two of them and their positions with the county they could easily frame him. Yes, it was the perfect plan.

She mulled ideas over and over in her mind for the rest of the morning. She finally made the bold and necessary decision to approach Louise about framing Rick. She walked over to her office and, without knocking walked in, shut the door behind her and sat down.

Louise raised her eyebrows at Cassie's boldness, but said nothing. The two sat there staring at each other for a moment, then Cassie spoke.

"I didn't have any luck at the Sheriff's Department getting Marne's cell phone. I managed to get into the evidence room and I saw a cubbyhole with her name on it, but there was no phone in it."

"Well, you've got to come up with a plan to either get your hands on that cell phone or see to it that the sheriff doesn't see the video. Have you come with anything, anything at all?"

"Well, yes, I have. Louise, I want to tell you something. This is hard for me to do, but I am at my wit's end trying to think of something that'll get me, and potentially all three of us, out of this mess. Louise, I've been having an affair with Rick. I know that your marriage hasn't been the best for the past year or so anyway, and he and I just sort of fell together."

"That son of a bitch!" said Louise. "I knew something was wrong. I knew it! Get the fuck out of my office NOW!"

"Louise, I'm sorry, I really am. But you would have to have been suspecting something with him. All those evenings he said that he was going back to the job sites to check on this and check on that . . . he was coming to see me. And you also have to admit that things have been over between you two for a while now, or at least going downhill. Y'all don't have any children together. You owned your house before you two ever got married, so there's nothing to be split up. He has been saying that he's going to file for divorce for the longest time. So I just figured that things were basically over between y'all anyway. Am I wrong?"

"Oh goddamn, Cassie, don't try to justify what you did! How could you do that to me? I thought we were friends. You've stabbed me right in the damn back. How long have you been seeing him?"

"A few months now, Louise."

"A few months. A few months. You are the sorriest excuse for a friend I've ever seen in my life, Cassie. And Rick, that piece of shit. And you're a piece of shit too, Cassie!"

Louise grew angrier and angrier, if that was possible, the longer she looked at Cassie as she pictured her husband lying on top of Cassie and pounding away at her. Finally, she exploded in an uncontrollable fit of rage. She stood up, slung her chair backwards on its rollers until it collided with the copy machine and knocked it over, spilling papers all over the floor. She grabbed a flower vase Rick had given to her on her birthday and slung it at Cassie, narrowly missing Cassie's head and exploding on the wall behind her, glass and water and flowers scattering everywhere.

The deputy clerks outside her office and two people standing at the counter to file cases heard the commotion coming from inside Louise's office and looked at her door. Finally, her chief deputy clerk timidly knocked on Louise's door and said, "Louise, is everything all right?" Louise?"

When she received no answer she slowly turned the knob and opened the door a few inches, just enough to see inside. The disarray of furniture and broken office equipment all over the floor made her gasp and pull back from the door opening.

"Louise, what's going on? What's wrong here?"

"Go tend to the office, Alethia, and mind your own business. This is between me and Cassie. Go. GO!"

Alethia stepped back from the door and closed it. She turned to the other office girls and they all stared at each other with wide eyes.

"What is it, what is it?" asked Margaret, the real estate clerk.

"They're having it out in there, but I don't know what about."

The couple who had come in to file some documents turned and left. The husband said to his wife, "I'll remember *this* next election year, you can bet on that."

Louise finally stood still for a moment, uprighted her chair, pulled it back to her desk which was now covered with scattered papers and sat back down. She cried with anger and the Cassie's betrayal, someone she had once considered her closest friend, her friend for life. Suddenly all of the good memories she had of their lunches together, their visits with each other in their offices, the times they went off together during work hours daring anybody to say anything to them, confiding their deepest secrets in each other were now gone.

"And Rick," she thought to herself. "That piece of shit, that goddamn piece of shit. I hate him. I swear I could cut his balls off right now."

Cassie pulled her chair back to face Louise and both of them became curiously quiet, but neither would make eye contact with the other. They just sat and stared away for what seemed like an eternity. Then, after Louise had finally calmed down and her tears began to subside a little, Cassie spoke.

"Louise, I actually came here with the original intention of suggesting something to you. I know you're mad right now, mad as hell. But I want you to put all this aside for a minute and think something through with me."

"Put all this aside?! Are you kidding me, you bitch?! You fuck my husband and then suggest that I should put my feelings aside about that?! What the hell!?"

"Louise, you've got every right to be upset, but we're dealing with a crisis too, one that we need to talk about no matter how mad you are at me right now."

Louise took a deep breath and finally looked directly at Cassie.

"All right. What is it you want to talk about that's so goddamn important?"

"Well, we've got Marne's murder and nobody's been charged with it. So I got to thinking . . . why don't we frame Rick for it? Then he'd be the patsy and the sheriff would be knee deep in the murder trial. We would all three be off the hook and you'd be out of a loveless marriage."

Louise wiped her eyes and threw the wet, balled-up tissue in the trash can with a thud.

"Maybe you've got something, Cassie. But let me think it over a little, huh? And please leave. I can't look at you right now. You've betrayed our friendship, fucked my husband, arranged a murder, and now to cover it up you want me to help you set up my husband as the murderer and send him to prison for the rest of his life for a crime he didn't commit. But then on the other hand, there's a part of me that doesn't really care what happens to him right now. That's a lot to think about."

Cassie nodded and walked towards Louise's office door. She put her hand on the knob but before she opened the door she turned once more to Louise and said, "We need to come up with a plan to set him up. Think about that too."

SHERIFF PORTIS CAME to Cassie's office unannounced and walked into the secretary's office, which was unmanned with the secretary out for some extended time off for the holiday.

"Judge?"

"Yes, come on in. I let my secretary have some time off this week, it being the week after Thanksgiving. What can I do for you?"

"I just wanted to follow up on our conversation from the other day about the fines and so forth."

"Oh, OK. What can I tell you about them?"

The sheriff decided to change his tactics. And the subject.

"Terrible about Marne Petakis, isn't it?"

"Huh? Oh, yes, terrible, sheriff. Any leads on who did it? I'm ready to grant arrest warrants any time y'all need them."

"Oh, I feel sure we'll have a suspect shortly. We're still working on it right now, of course, but we're beginning to narrow down our list some."

Suspects? Narrowing down your list? Cassie swallowed hard at the sheriff's words, trying not to show any reaction.

"Of course. I know these things take time."

"Yes, they do. But we've got some real good leads. I think we'll be ready to make an arrest in the next couple of days or so."

"Really? That soon?"

"Oh, yeah. We've determined the angle of the shot, where the shooter was hiding, what kind of gun he or she used; we've even recovered the shell casing and the bullet. We've made a lot of progress."

Cassie tried to hide her reaction to the sheriff's news and especially his politically-correct wording of "he *or she*". If they grab that damn Harry Blakely, there's no telling what that dumbass might tell them about her. Hell, he'd probably spill his guts about the whole damn thing.

"Well, you just let me know how I can help on my end, sheriff. I'll be glad when you nab that bastard. What a brutal killing. Being shot to death in your own yard. Horrible."

"Yeah, it was pretty bad. One of the worst crime scenes I've ever seen, and I've seen a lot of them. And you know, judge, she had so many enemies in this town. So many enemies. She always seemed to be at odds with somebody, no matter whether they had done anything wrong or not. Why, just take this situation with your fines being down. That's the very kind of thing she would really have gone off the deep end over. Money, money, money, that was her thing. Get the county coffers up, you know? Just make sure that taxes are as low as they can possibly be on the one hand, but that money coming in from other sources is as high as possible on the other. Like fines, for instance. She thought that everybody who spits on the sidewalk ought to have to pay a million dollar fine. Yes, she definitely wanted the county to do well financially without the taxpayers having to pay anything to it. That was her interest, her passion, her crack cocaine. Well, anyway, I get off the subject. Sorry. So, judge, on the subject of fines, there are some people who are curious about how the numbers of defendants have increased but the fines have decreased. I think that she was just, I mean, that *they're* just chasing rainbows myself, but I did promise that I'd at least ask about them."

Cassie couldn't help but notice how the sheriff was choosing his words. Was he putting things the way he was putting them by accident or on purpose?

"Well, like I explained before, I just don't want to gouge anybody over minor offenses. That darn Chris Harper used to levy exorbitant fines on these poor old folks who, as you surely know, simply can't afford to be paying out huge amounts of money. I just feel it's my duty as their judge to not punish them excessively regardless of what Marne thinks. Thought. That's all."

"Well, of course, I didn't say that Marne had complained about you specifically, judge. As always, I appreciate your time. I think you've explained everything about as well as I could expect. I hope you had a happy Thanksgiving."

"You as well, sheriff. Thank you for coming by."

The sheriff left and Cassie's worrisome thoughts again invaded her evil little mind.

"A suspect? Who?"

The Affair

Louise sat stewing in her own thoughts in her office chair for quite a while after Cassie had left. How could Rick do that to her? That bastard. That goddamn bastard.

But she couldn't ignore Cassie's suggestion of blaming the murder on him. If their marriage was pretty much over anyway, what better way to get rid of him and get the sheriff off the trail of looking into Cassie's fines, Angelina's fines and possible her own skimming operations? She eventually decided to call her husband's mistress.

"Magistrate Court."

"Hey, it's me. Can you come back down here? I want to talk to you some more about your idea."

"Yeah, as a matter of fact I need to talk to you too. Sheriff Portis just left here."

"What the hell did he want?"

"I'll tell you when I get there."

Cassie went into Louise's office and shut the door behind her, weaving her way around the mess in the floor to reach the chair.

"He said that he had a few suspects in mind, Louise. What if one of them is me?"

"What makes you think he's interested in you as a suspect?"

"Well, he sure is taking a lot of interest in my fines and why the amounts are down so much. This is the second time he's asked me about them. And if he's on to me then it's very likely he's on to Angelina and you too. We talked a little about Marne's murder just in conversation and he made a really cryptic remark about how my fines being so low is the very type of thing she would've complained about. But that's all he would say, like he was saying it just to get my reaction. If Marne was the one who got him started investigating then that gives me a motive."

Just then Louise's phone rang.

"Clerk's Office."

"Hey, it's me," said Angelina. "Guess who was just here?"

"Who?"

"Sheriff Portis."

"Can you come over here?"

"On my way."

Angelina Black walked into Louise's office and took a seat.

"You two look like a gruesome twosome."

"Well, you don't make us a thrillsome threesome," said Louise. "What was Portis wanting?"

"What do you think? He was asking me why my fines are lower than they used to be when there are more cases than before. I'm getting real nervous, y'all. Real nervous."

Louise and Cassie looked at each other.

"Yeah," said Louise, "he keeps asking Cassie a lot of questions too. He's talked to her a couple of times now. I think it's just a matter of time before he starts looking into my figures too. We've got a lot to talk about."

"You're goddamn right about that," replied Angelina.

"Okay," began Louise, let's take a look at what we've got. First, Sheriff Portis shows all this interest in Cassie's fines. Second, he now comes to you and asks you the same type of questions he's been asking Cassie. Third, and you ain't gonna believe this one, Cassie dropped a bombshell on me a little while ago. She's been fucking Rick."

Angelina's eyes opened wide as she looked at Cassie. "What?!"

"Oh, yeah. Rick's been cheating on me for how long, Cassie?"

"About four or five months," answered Cassie sheepishly.

Angelina looked at Cassie. "Cassie, what the hell?!"

"Oh, it pisses me off to no end, Angelina, but hold on," interjected Louise. "Cassie has an idea. Tell her, Cassie."

"I think the sheriff is focusing on me with this damn Marne Petakis murder. The way I see it, she's probably the one who reported these discrepancies with my fines in the first place, which gives me a motive for having her killed. I think we should figure out a way to pin the murder on Rick. That would solve all the problems for all of us. That would completely divert the sheriff's attention away from anything we're doing and focus everything on Rick being involved in Marne's murder. And arresting the husband of the clerk of court and charging him with murder would definitely stir up a media circus too. Just think about it. And while this is going on we could all pull our operations back a little, slow down some. Remember, you two have been doing the same thing I have. I think that eventually, the sheriff is going to put two and two together. It's been a really sweet gig so far, but what happens if he starts asking questions of some of our defendants that we've scammed? Once the murder investigation and trial are over, we could resume normal operations." Cassie took a drink of water and thought for a moment. "The sheriff says they've recovered both the bullet and the shell casing. I don't know if they really have or if he's just trying to feel me out to see my reaction. I need to talk to Blakely."

CASSIE DROVE INTO HARRY Blakely's yard to find him outside smoking and drinking a beer in the yard. She eased the car into the meager space in his driveway and got out.

"Well, you again," he said, little in the way of a welcoming tone in his voice. "What's up now? You want somebody else killed?"

"Hush, goddamnit, lower your voice! You want to get us caught?!"

"Oh, ain't a damn soul gonna hear us. What's on your mind this time?"

"I need to ask you something. Can we go inside?"

"Oh, let's just talk out here. Sit down." He pointed to a chair in about the same shape as his porch. Cassie carefully sat down, hoping that her weight wouldn't shatter it and put her on the ground underneath it flat on her ass.

"Sorry for the condition of my lawn furniture, but I'm got some brand new stuff on order. Courtesy of Marne Petakis."

"After you shot Marne did you get anything of hers, specifically, her cell phone?"

"No, you never said nothing about a cell phone."

"That's what I thought. Let me ask you this: After you shot did you cock your gun and eject the shell?"

"No. I made it a point to put her down with one shot so I wouldn't need to cock it again. I cocked the lever in my car on the way back here and threw the casing out the window. It's long gone."

"Are you sure?"

"One hundred percent sure, Miss Manson. Remember, this ain't my first rodeo."

"OK. I just wanted to make sure the sheriff didn't recover the casing."

"He couldn't have. It's laying on the side of the road somewhere between here and there. It's gone, believe me."

"Good. What kind of a gun did you use?"

"Why the hell are you asking so many questions, Miss Manson?"

"Believe me, Mr. Blakely, I'm not trying to get you into anything. The truth is that I'm trying to keep you and me both from any suspicion at all."

"Well, I used my .30-.30. I mentioned that when you were here before. Why?"

"I've got a plan on how to pin this on somebody else. You'd be glad of that, wouldn't you, Mr. Blakely? The authorities prosecute somebody else for the crime and leave both you and me alone forever?"

Blakely took another swig of beer and smiled. "Hell, yeah! That's a plan for sure."

"Where did you shoot her from? I mean, where were you standing?"

"Right across the road from the front of her house. Her mailbox and driveway were a little to my right as I was facing the house."

"Thank you, Mr. Blakely. Enjoy your money."

With that Cassie got back into her car and left, hoping to never see this man again.

CASSIE IMMEDIATELY called Louise after she left Blakely's house.

"Hello."

"Louise, I just visited Blakely and I've got good news and bad news. The bad news is that he didn't get her cell phone. The good news is that he said said he made it a point to not cock his rifle at the scene so that he wouldn't leave any shell casings. He cocked it in his car on his way back home and threw it out on the side of the road. So it'll never be found or connected with the murder!"

"That's great, Cassie. So where do we go from here about Rick?"

"Doesn't Rick deer hunt?"

"Yes."

"What kind of a gun does he use?"

"He's got several, but his favorite is his .30-.30."

"A .30-.30. Perfect! That's what Blakely said he used. Can you get a hold of one of Rick's shells?"

"Yes."

"Do you know how to shoot it?"

"Yeah, I can shoot it. Why?"

"Here's what I want you to do, Louise. I want you to shoot it, eject the empty shell, clean it off and then somehow get him to touch it. We need his fingerprints on it."

"OK. But what would Rick's motive be for murdering Marne?"

"I don't know. Maybe something that made him have a grudge against her? Do you know if he knew her, or ever even met her?"

"He knows who she was, but I don't think he's ever had any dealings with her. The only thing he ever said about her was how she was such a busybody, reporting people for nothing, always trying to get people fired for things whether they did anything wrong or not. To my knowledge the only time he ever even spoke to her was at the grocery store once when he came home complaining about how she confronted him about some environmental violations she thought he was committing, something about dirt and mud runoff from lawns he was working on."

"Oh, yeah? What all did she say to him?"

"Well, it wasn't much, really. He said that he was on his way out and she was coming in and she said something to him, something like 'Hey, don't you run that landscaping business? Well, you sure do flirt with a lot of violations with that massive dirt and mud runoff at people's yards you're working on.'" He just sort of shrugged it off and basically told her to go screw herself, although knowing Rick I'm not sure those were his exact words."

"Well, maybe that's something we can use. How about this – you dummy up something to show that she was going to report him for it. I don't see any reason that we couldn't do that. You could write some letters and take them to the sheriff."

"You mean write letters that are from her, then something back to her from him, and so forth?"

"Yes! Get to work on it when you get home. I'm excited, Louise. I think this whole thing is going to come together for us all!"

WHEN LOUISE GOT HOME she made a beeline for the home computer in Rick's little room that he uses as an office. She thought for a while, then began to write:

"Dear Mr. Ambrose:

It has been brought to my attention that your company, Rick's Landscaping & Grading, has been engaged in some practices which are offensive to the citizens of Jasper County and downright destructive to the environment. I have personally seen many examples of drainage runoff and excessive ground dirt and mud washing into roads adjacent to the properties whose yards you are working on. It is my intention to bring this to the attention of the proper authorities, but I would be willing to forgo such actions if you will correct the problems immediately.

Please be advised that fines and penalties for such violations can be quite substantial. It would be much more advantageous for you to simply comply with federal, state and county laws that govern the environmental aspects of your work, and I hope that you will do so rather than see this matter escalate to a higher level.

Please govern yourself accordingly.

Sincerely,

Marne Petakis"

"Oh, that's brilliant," said Louise to herself. She then typed up many more letters, some from Marne and some from Rick.

"Dear Ms. Petakis:

I am in receipt of your letter falsely accusing me of acting in a manner which is in violation of environmental laws. I can assure you that my company operates well within the parameters of all laws, ordinances and statutes of Jasper County, the state of Georgia and federal mandates in its landscaping and related operations. If you have seen runoff from my job sites it was likely caused by rain following my tilling and scraping of lawns and yards to bring them to the customers' specifications and expectations. There is naturally going to be some dirty water and light mud flowing from such operations. This is natural and does not continue once the grass begins to grow on the lawns.

Therefore, Ms. Petakis, I see no reason for any further "escalation", as you put it, of this matter and I suggest that you direct your hostilities and vitriol towards those more deserving of your efforts, which you are well known to do.

I consider the matter closed.

Sincerely,

Richard K. Ambrose"

"Oh, that's great too!" exclaimed Louise out loud. Her hubris had no limits now. Not only had she found out that Rick was cheating on her, but she and Cassie had concocted an elaborate plan to frame him for the murder of their enemy and all of her plans would result in their embezzlement scheme being forgotten. "Yesterday's newspaper in today's trash can."

She took the letters and carefully put them in a stack of courthouse papers to bring to work the next day.

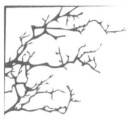

The Setup

The next morning Cassie went directly to her office. She stormed in and nodded at her secretary without saying a word.

"Is something wrong, judge?"

"Huh? Uh, no. Just a lot on my mind today, Amy."

"Yes, ma'am. Well, I've got some court orders for you to sign at your convenience."

"Hand them to me."

Cassie took the papers and closed her inner office door. Later that morning Louise called her and told her she had something to show her. Cassie walked down to Louise's office, went in, closed the door and sat down.

"I've got those letters I wrote up between Rick and Marne, Cassie. Here, take a look at them."

Cassie took the papers from Louise and read them over.

"These are fantastic, Louise! Now all we need to do is figure out a way to get these in the hands of the sheriff, and I think I've got a way. If I'm careful, I could go to her house and put them in her desk drawer. She worked from home , so you know she had some sort of office space in her house. I could put them under something that would make it look like the deputies simply missed them the first time they searched."

"That's a great idea, if risky. You figure you can pull that off without getting caught?"

"Yeah, I think so. Have you fired the gun yet?"

"No, not yet. I'll do that sometime today. Have you thought about how we're going to get the sheriff to find the shell casing?"

"Louise, I can't think of everything myself!" retorted Cassie. "You're going to have to come up with something too! Think. Just think."

Louise could see that this entire matter was taking its emotional toll on Cassie, so she brushed her aside and said, "Just go back to your office and let me see if I can come up with something, something that'll work. It's got to be foolproof."

Cassie nodded and left Louise's office.

LOUISE WENT HOME AT lunchtime to an empty house, Rick at a job site and the children in school.

She went to his gun cabinet and picked through his array of rifles, making sure that she picked up the right one, his Marlin .30-.30. After some perusing through the ammunition box she found the right bullets and put one in the chamber. She walked outside and went down into the woods at the back of their property, cocked the rifle, pulled back the hammer and fired the weapon at a tree, the bullet spewing splinters of wood from its impact. She cringed a little at how a weapon just like this one had split Marne Petakis' head in two, spilling her brains all over the driveway, knocking out her eyeball, the jolt causing her to bite her tongue off. Yes, she must've been a mess if the description she had read in the sheriff's incident report was any indication.

But this must be done. Her embezzlement scheme, one she had engaged in along with the other two women, could not be compromised or discovered. The county sheriff, that straight-as-an-arrow lawman, would not hesitate to arrest and prosecute all three of them if he thought they were involved in the crimes they were now mired in. She smiled at having accomplished her task and went back into the house, shell in hand, and carefully put the rifle back into its cabinet.

When she returned to the courthouse she stopped by Cassie's office.

"I shot the gun a little while ago and got the empty shell. I wiped it down and put it in my pocketbook. Now I've got to get Rick to put his hands on it. I'll do something tonight after supper."

DINNER WAS PLACED ON the Ambrose dinner table as usual that night. Rick and the children ate and talked, talked and ate, and eventually supper was finished.

"That was delicious, Louise. Thank you." Rick stood to leave the table.

"Oh, sit back down, honey," urged Louise. "I want to ask you something."

"Shoot."

Louise cracked a slight grin at the irony of Rick's expression. "Are you going hunting any more this season?"

"Yeah, I thought I would. Why? Did you have something else planned?"

"Oh no, not at all. In fact I want you to go. I loved that deer meat from last year. I'm disappointed that you haven't gotten one this season yet."

"Well, this is the first hunting season when I've had my own business, which is taking up a lot more of my time than before. You know I'm often gone off on Saturdays, but maybe this weekend I can go. Matt said I could hunt on his land, said it's crawling with deer."

Louise thought to herself, "Yeah, and it takes a lot of time to fuck that fat magistrate too, doesn't it?," but she bit her tongue.

"I want you to teach me how to shoot. Maybe I can go with you some time. Hold on, let me go get your gun."

Louise went to the gun cabinet and brought back the .30-.30 rifle that she had shot earlier.

"I found this empty shell in the backyard from where you were target practicing before the season started. Can you show me how to load it and everything?"

"Well, yeah, but let's use a live round. We don't need to put a spent bullet shell in the gun."

"Oh, no, not in the house, Rick. Just use this one that's empty."

"Well, OK. But I wouldn't shoot anybody, I promise."

Louise laughed at the ironic humor she found in Rick's comment. "Oh, but yes you did, don't you know you shot Marne Petakis, you son of a bitch?" she thought to herself.

"Here, let me wash it and dry it. Wouldn't want to get any dirt in your gun."

"Good thinking."

Louise washed the bullet shell in the kitchen sink and wiped it down thoroughly, giving her an excuse to use a napkin to hold it when handing it to Rick.

"Well, you see, it's not hard to load at all. You just push it in the little slot on the side, then cock it with the lever. When you first cock it it puts the hammer back, meaning it's ready to shoot, so be careful to release it when you do that. But then you have to pull the hammer back when you want to shoot it."

"So how do you get the bullet shell out after you've fired it?"

Rick's answer was to cock the lever again and she watched as the shell shot out of the top of the rifle and onto the floor. Rick reached down and picked it up, Louise carefully watching to make sure he held it in such a way as to leave as many fingerprints on it as possible. Satisfied, she leaned back in her chair to indicate that the lesson was over.

"Thanks, Rick. Maybe sometime you can show me how to actually shoot it."

"That'd be fine." Rick then left the table and returned his rifle to the cabinet, tossing the spent shell casing in the trash can in his den. He casually walked out to his shop while Louise hurriedly grabbed a tissue and picked up the shell, putting it in a sandwich bag and sealing the top.

"Exhibit 'A,'" she said.

LOUISE WENT TO CASSIE'S office the next morning with a big, wide grin on her face.

"What's up? You look happy."

Louanne held up the sandwich bag. "Look, I got the shell casing and Rick touched it. His fingerprints should be all over it. Now we've got to plan the next step."

"Okay, said Cassie, "How about this – You call the sheriff and tell him that you've found out that Rick might be in trouble with the EPA or something. Tell him that Rick casually mentioned something about a bunch of letters between him and Marne arguing back and forth about how he's polluting the roads and such, something like that. Ask the sheriff what he thinks about the letters, suggesting that you presume that they found them at Marne's house, and when he says that they never found any, tell him that it might be a good idea for him to go back and another look. Tell him that you're worried that Rick might have had something to do with Marne's murder and your conscience won't let you stand by and do nothing. In the meantime I'll take the letters and that bullet over to Marne's house. I'll get inside somehow and plant the letters, then toss the casing into the bushes near where Blakely said he shot from. You put a bug in the sheriff's ear about Rick having a .30-.30 and other high-powered rifles and that while he's at Marne's looking for the letters, maybe he should take another look at the crime scene to see if he can find a shell. I'll put it in a place where it'll definitely be found, but hidden away enough so that they'll think they just overlooked it before."

"Wow, sounds like you've really thought this through, Cassie. Yeah, let's try it.."

CASSIE DROVE DOWN THE country road towards Marne's now-unoccupied house and pulled off onto the shoulder several yards away. She nervously looked all around to make sure she wasn't seen and that no cars were coming which, on that isolated road could be heard approaching from a long way off. Confident that she was alone and unseen, she walked up to the house and knocked on the door. She held her breath in the expectation that no one would answer the door and indeed, she had heard that no one was living there since the murder. She walked around to the back of the house and shouted "Is anyone home? Hello?"

No response. Nothing. Not even a dog barking. She figured that Marne's son must've taken the dog after she was murdered.

She edged her way up to the back patio door and cupped her hands around her eyes to look inside. Again, no one. No lights on. No ceiling fans spinning. No sign of life. No activity.

She first tugged on the sliding glass patio door, hoping that luck would be on her side and it might, just might, have been left unlocked. It was locked. She took out a credit card and slid it in between the door and the metal strip it fit into. "Come on, I've done this before," she said out loud. "Unlock, damn you."

Somewhat to her surprise, the door latch slid up. It was now unlocked. She pulled one of her ever-present tissues out and wrapped it around her fingers, grabbed the handled and pulled.

The door was open.

She quickly closed the door behind her and turned around. She was very taken at how pristine the place was. She had somehow pictured Marne to be an eccentric woman with clothes hanging on the backs of chairs, empty coffee cups on the table, dust everywhere. But this house was immaculate.

She wandered through the house, careful not to touch anything. When she entered into a room she used the tissues like she had done when she first came in through the sliding glass door. She perused through the third room she had entered and she saw a desk, some books stacked neatly on shelves and a computer.

"Jackpot!"

She carefully opened the bottom drawer of the desk and saw a few manila folders and envelopes. She took out the letters Louise had prepared and lifted up the various items in the drawer, placing the letters underneath. She carefully put the folders and papers back, closed the desk, ever mindful to touch things with her tissue-wrapped fingers and stood there, spending a moment to stare at her wicked accomplishment. She turned to leave with a wry smile on her face and began walking towards the patio door.

Then she heard a car drive up.

Panic began to set in. She started breathing heavily, almost to the point of passing out. She looked for the nearest closet and ran towards it, opened the door, and slipped inside.

Who could it be? The sheriff?

The key inserted into the front door lock made that unmistakable sound of metal on metal. She heard the click of the latch. The doorknob turned and the door opened. She heard footsteps going across the living room floor, her heart racing and thumping in her chest with every step. She prayed that whoever it was would not come into that part of the house, as if God would have an interest in protecting someone so evil and twisted.

She had left the door to the bedroom-turned-office open, and as the person walked down the short hallway towards it she sank down into some of the dead lady's clothes in a neat stack in the back of the closet. She tried to find something to cover herself with should he or she open the closet door, but in the darkness could find nothing. Then she heard a voice. A man's voice.

"I could have sworn I closed all these doors, especially this one. I'm sorry, mama."

It was Marne's son, Justin. What the hell was he doing here? And of all the times! If he's going through her things, cleaning the place out, taking inventory, she's toast. Then she heard him begin speaking again."

"Hey, this is Justin Petakis. I don't see anything with your name on it. When you were here did you see what she put it in? I presume she used a manila folder, but maybe she used something else. Oh. Oh, okay. Let me look in the other file cabinet. Does it tie at the top? Accordion-type? Oh, you mean one of those extra thick folder things."

Then she heard him open a file cabinet next to the closet.

"Ah, here it is. It's labeled 'Stancell Investments'. That's got to be it. I'll bring it over tomorrow afternoon if that's all right. You're welcome. Thank you, that's very kind of you. Yes, her death was certainly a blow to us all. The entire county is in shock. Oh yes, many friends. Many, many friends. I don't think the church sanctuary will be able to hold all the grieving people. She was so well-loved here. Day after tomorrow. Right, the one right there in town next to the ballfield. Two o'clock. Yes, that would work. I'll bring your file and I can just give it to you at the funeral. You, too. Good-bye."

Justin then closed the file drawer, tucked the folder under his arm and walked back into the living room and out of the house. Cassie breathed a heavy sigh of relief when she heard the car crank and back out of the driveway and out onto the road.

"My God. That was close."

She did take a moment to cringe at Justin telling the person on the other end of the phone how well-loved Marne was, so much so that the church might not be able to hold all the mourners. Ha!

She edged her way to the closet door, fumbling to find the knob and finally opening the door. She slowly walked out into the room and into the living room, peering out the window to make double sure that the coast was clear. When she was convinced that it was safe to leave, she went back out the sliding glass patio door, pushed it shut, and locked it with her credit card. Once outside she looked all around again and walked across the street to the spot where Blakely said he parked when he did the deed. She trudged her way a few feet into the bushes, noticing the boot prints from the deputies in the soft dirt. She found a log, not too big and not too small and picked it up, carefully removed the shell casing from the sandwich bag, and maneuvered it into the exact position she wanted it in. She placed the log on top of it, looked all around one last time to make sure she wasn't seen, and wasted no time in returning to her car, calling Louise as soon as she was behind the wheel.

"Hello."

"It's me. It's done. Time to get in touch with Sheriff Portis."

LOUISE ARRIVED AT THE sheriff's department late that afternoon. She had done all she could to manufacture an appearance of worry and guilt at reporting her husband to the sheriff, pulling on her days of drama class in high school for as much fake drama as she could muster. She told the sheriff's secretary that she needed to see the sheriff and that it was urgent.

"Hello, Louise. Please, come in. What brings you out this way today?"

"Sheriff, I have something I want to tell you about that is very difficult for me. I must confess that I don't really know how to tell you this."

"My goodness, Louise, calm down and have a seat. Can I get you anything, a drink of water maybe? Are you all right? Is everything okay?"

"Yes, some water would be great, please, sheriff. I'm so distraught right now I don't know what to do!"

The sheriff poured Louise a cup of water to the sound of the gurgling in the water cooler and handed it to her.

"All right, now first I want you to just calm down just a little bit for me, okay? Take a deep breath for a second. That's better, that's better. Whatever it is I'm sure we can work it out. Now tell me what happened."

"Sheriff Portis, I am deeply disturbed by something Rick told me last night. He said that he and Marne Petakis had some rather hostile dealings recently. He said that she had been accusing him of some sort of environmental violations, that they've been sending some very sternly-worded letters back and forth to each other for a while. Rick mentioned to me that she had confronted him at the grocery store in town about it, but that was pretty much all he said about it. He never told me about any letters or anything. I don't know if he was really violating some sort of environmental rules or if he just didn't want me to worry about anything, or what. I just know that he had a run-in with her over this stuff, and then she turns up dead. Sheriff, I'm worried to death that my husband might have had something to do with, with..."

"All right, Louise, let's just take a minute to think about this. Even if he and Marne didn't see eye to eye on something, that could be said of a lot of people where she was concerned. I'm sorry to say it this way, but she wasn't exactly the most well-liked person in the county, God rest her soul."

Louise began to become concerned that the sheriff wasn't taking the bait. Her drama class training kicked up a notch and she began to cry crocodile tears.

"But sheriff, I don't know what to make of all this! My God, I don't want to be living with a murderer!"

"Now, Louise, it's a pretty big leap from them sending hostile letters back and forth to murder, you have to admit. I know you're upset that he didn't tell you about the extent of this, but let's not jump the gun here."

"Oh, sheriff," she said as the tears continued to flow, "I don't know what to do. What if I'm sleeping in the same bed with a man who blew a woman's head in two with a rifle?! I can't say that I liked Marne any more than anybody else, but this is something different altogether. Murder? Really? My husband? Oh, sheriff."

She feigned momentarily regaining her composure.

"What exactly did the letters say, sheriff? I'm sure you confiscated them from her house after the murder."

"Well, no, Louise, this is the first I've heard of them. Rick didn't show them to you himself?"

"No, he said that he destroyed his copies out of anger. He said that he told her something about considering the matter closed."

"I tell you what. I'll make a deal with you, Louise. You let me take a look through her things again to see if I can find her copies of these letters. Then I'll go talk to him. Fair enough?"

"Oh, that would be great, sheriff. I feel sure she kept the ones he sent to her and copies of the ones she sent to him. But if you do conclude that he had something to do with this horrible crime you will protect me, won't you? I mean, if he finds out that I'm the one who told you about this, who knows what he might do? If he can kill Marne Petakis he can kill me!"

"He's not going to hurt you, Louise. And I promise I'll get to the bottom of this. Now, I want you to go home, relax, and just let me do my job. Okay?"

"Of course, sheriff. Just promise me you'll protect me from him if things go bad. I mean, he's a hunter and he's got all those guns. I'm just worried, that's all."

"You have my word. Now, what's his cell phone number?"

Louise reined in her tears she had cried for the sheriff's benefit. After a few moments she gave him Rick's cell phone number, stood up, thanked him and turned to leave. As she was about to shut the door behind her the sheriff spoke.

"Oh, Louise, one more thing."

"Yes, Dave?"

"Marne was killed on the Monday before Thanksgiving late in the evening. Where was Rick at that time, if you remember?"

"Let me see, the Monday before Thanksgiving. Hmm. The Monday before... Oh, I know. He was at home for supper and for a little while afterwards, but then he left out to go to a job site to check on some grass seed or something."

The sheriff nodded his thanks and Louise left, thinking to herself how convenient it had been that he left that evening, even if it was Cassie's house he went to.

The Smoking Gun

Sheriff Portis drove up into Marne Petakis' yard amid the still-present yellow "Crime Scene" tape that surrounded the property. It gave him a strange feeling to be standing feet away from where a woman lost her life only days earlier. He opened the front door with the key her son had provided him with and walked to her home office. He opened each desk drawer one by one and went through the contents of each, finding nothing in the way of correspondence between Rick and Marne. Finally, he opened the last one and thumbed through the papers stacked in it. He was just about to put them back when he saw a letter with Rick Ambrose's company letterhead. He turned on the light on her desk as he read each one.

"So, Louise was right. He was having a bit of a row with Marne.'"

The sheriff took an empty manila folder from a stack on the desk and placed the letters inside.

"Hmm. Wonder what else we missed?"

The sheriff walked outside, locking the door on his way out, stopped by his car and put the folder containing the incriminating letters on the passenger's seat. He walked around to the driver's door, opened it, and stood for a moment looking at the presumed shooter's nest. He put one foot inside the car to leave, stood there scanning the spot, and then slowly got inside his car and left. But on his way out the driveway he mumbled to himself, "We must've missed something. We *must* have."

"RICK'S GRADING."

"Rick?"

"Yes."

"Dave Portis. How're you?"

"Sheriff! Long time. I'm fine, thanks. You?"

"Doing well, thanks. Rick, I wonder if you could spare a few minutes to meet with me? I've got something I want to go over with you and I promise I won't take up too much of your time."

"Well, sure, sheriff. When did you have in mind?"

"Are you busy at the moment?"

"I'm just finishing up a job site, loading up my equipment. You want me to come by the department? I'm not that far away right now, actually."

"If you don't mind, I'd appreciate that. I'll be looking for you in what, half an hour or so?"

"That sounds about right. See you then."

"Thanks, Rick."

The two hung up the phone as Rick pondered what the sheriff could possibly want to talk to him about. He arrived at the sheriff's department and went to Dave Portis' office, first apologizing for his unkempt appearance.

"Oh, don't you worry about that at all, Rick," said the sheriff as they shook hands. "I know that's hard work you do out there. I need to do a little yardwork myself, actually."

Rick chuckled nervously as he sat down in front of the sheriff's desk. During the entire drive there he had combed through his mind like a student summoned to the principal's office, wondering why he's being asked to come there as he made the long walk down the hallway.

"Rick, I was going through some of Marne Petakis' things and I found . . . I presume you've heard about her?"

"Oh, yeah, terrible thing, even for somebody who enjoyed stirring up as much crap as she did. I swear, I don't think there was a person in the county who liked her. You never saw her with anybody else, always by herself, always alone. I think her dog must've been her only friend in the world."

The sheriff made a mental note that Marne had a photo of her with her dog as her cell phone home screen. How did Rick know that she had a dog?

"Yeah, I know what you mean, Rick. Well, anyway, I know there had been some bad blood between you two going back and forth about this environmental stuff. I'm sure in your business you probably get flak from people from time to time about different things, water runoff, mud seeping onto the road, gravel getting on people's streets, things like that. But this thing between you and Marne seemed to be pretty hostile."

"I'm not sure I know what you mean, sheriff. What environmental stuff?"

"The letters you two exchanged about her threatening to report you to the EPA and so on."

"Uh, I never had any letters going back and forth with her about anything. She made some smart ass remark to me as I was going in the grocery store one time, but that was it. I haven't had any contact with her of any kind before or since then."

The sheriff leaned back in his chair and furrowed his eyebrows.

"Oh, is that right? I've got some letters here that you two exchanged, copies she sent to you and the originals of your responses."

"May I see them?"

"Sure," said the sheriff as he handed the stack of about thirty letters to Rick. Rick began to thumb through them, reading each one a little faster than the one before.

"Sheriff, these aren't mine. I never sent these letters with my letterhead on them nor saw the ones from her."

"Rick, are you sure? I found them in her desk drawer. What else would they be?"

"I have no idea, sheriff."

"So you have never seen these letters before?"

"That's correct."

"None of them?"

"None."

Have you ever been reported to any environmental authorities?"

"Never."

"Well, that's a mystery, isn't it?" The sheriff decided not to pursue the matter of the letters any further and turned his attention to another thing that had piqued his interest.

"Have you ever been to her house?"

"Can't say that I have."

"How much do you know about her?"

"Oh, I don't know much about her at all, just who she was but in this county, who didn't? She was always plastering her face on the front page of the newspaper or social media with some gripe about this person or that person. That seemed to be her whole reason for living, to see how many people's lives she could destroy. But I'm sure she herself was perfect. Isn't that how those people think? 'Everybody in the world is a guilty of everything except me.'"

"Well, for somebody who didn't know her you sure have a lot of vitriol to say about her."

"I don't mean to sound that way, sheriff, honestly I don't. I just didn't like how she always presumed that somebody had done something wrong and then tried to find something to justify her conclusion. And with Louise being in the courthouse I was always worried that she might be next."

"Well, Rick, I'm going to be honest with you. These letters indicate a long-running hostility between you and Marne, then she is murdered. Now, I don't have any reason to suspect you of something like that, but when I see letters like this I have an obligation to check into them. Can you tell me where you were on the Monday night before Thanksgiving at around nine or ten o'clock?"

Rick remembered that he was in bed with Cassie at the time of the murder, and he suddenly became defensive.

"Am I a friggin' suspect in a murder, Dave? What the hell?!"

"Calm down, Rick. I'm just asking questions, that's all. I've got to check out everything. So do you remember where you were?"

Rick began to shake with nervousness. His voice quivered as he searched his mind to remember which job site he had been working on earlier that day before he went to his mistress' house, who just happens to be the damn judge.

"Uh, I was at a job site."

"At that hour?"

"Yeah, well, sometimes that's necessary. We put down grass seed and cover it with hay and straw and then if it's supposed to rain I like to make sure that it's all in place so it doesn't wash away."

"Well, couldn't you make sure of that before you leave the job site for the day while it's daylight?"

"Well, you see, sheriff, the wind blows the straw around a lot, so I need to go back as close to the time before it starts raining as I can to make sure it's still in place. Otherwise I might come back the next day and see a yard half filled with exposed grass seed and the other half in the road."

"Of course. I hadn't thought about that. So you were at this job site?"

"Yes."

"Which one?"

Rick had to think fast. "Out on Highway 11 near Hillsboro."

"Was anybody with you?"

"No, it was just me. I wouldn't want to ask any of my employees to come out to a job site at such an hour unless it was an emergency."

"What time did you get there?"

"Must've been around eight or nine o'clock."

"How long did you stay?"

"I figure I was out there a couple of hours."

"Must've been a big yard."

"Oh yeah, pretty big."

"Where on Highway 11?"

"Uh, just down near Hillsboro, sheriff. Not far from the town limits on the north side."

"If I go down there can I find it?"

Rick started to sweat. Now what was he going to tell the sheriff? He was no where near Hillsboro at a job site; he was fucking the magistrate judge. If he admitted that to the sheriff Louise would be sure to find out, not to mention the scandalous maelstrom that would be created by revealing such a thing. He had to think fast, again.

"You know, sheriff, I just remembered. That wasn't the Hillsboro site, that was the Mansfield site. Some new house up there on Highway 11 just before you get to Mansfield. Sorry I first said Hillsboro but then again, it has been a few days ago."

"Oh, I see. Not Hillsboro but Mansfield."

"Right."

The sheriff decided to play it coy.

"Well, thank you for coming in, Rick. I appreciate your time. Hey, you got you a deer yet?"

"No, not yet. Planning on going this weekend maybe, though."

"Yeah, me too. I've got to sight in my rifle first. Ain't that a shame? Here I am, the high sheriff with guns galore and an avid hunter, and I haven't even been hunting this season yet? You know, hunting season doesn't last all that long. And we are the Deer Capital of Georgia, as they say."

"Yeah, Louise was telling me how she misses the venison. Properly cured and butchered, it makes great steaks."

"Yeah, makes me hungry just talking about it. I've got a real nice .308 with a scope. What do you use?"

"Well, I've got several deer rifles, but my favorite is my Marlin .30-.30. I've dropped many a buck with that baby."

"Well, good hunting, Rick. Again, thanks for coming in."

Rick and the sheriff stood to shake hands.

"Oh, it's my pleasure, sheriff. I hope you and yours are enjoying the holiday season."

"Thank you. Same to you"

Rick then turned and headed for the door, wasting no time in getting out of the sheriff's office before another question could be asked. But he didn't make it.

"Oh, Rick, one more thing, if I may."

"Sure."

"You, uh, say you've never been to Marne's house?"

"Never."

"Didn't know her personally, anything about her personal life?"

"Not a thing."

"How did you know she had a dog?"

"I beg your pardon?"

"Well, earlier you said that her dog was probably her only friend. I tend to agree, by the way." The two cracked a smile at the sheriff's effort to inject some humor into what had been a conversation Rick had been noticeably apprehensive about.

"But seriously, how *did* you know she had dog?"

"I just figured somebody like her would need man's best friend, or I guess it would be woman's best friend, or in her case woman's only friend. Who else would she have?"

"Yeah, I guess you're right. She would love that dog to death, at least until he did something she didn't like and she turned on him and started writing bad things about him in the newspaper and on social media."

Rick laughed as he left the sheriff's office, got in his truck and left.

Sheriff Portis now had a suspect. He needed to visit the crime scene again.

SHERIFF PORTIS DROVE to Marne's house, the scene of the grisly murder just days earlier. Just being where such a horrible crime had taken place gave him a chill beyond that caused by the crisp November air. But he was a professional lawman with a job to do so he put his emotions aside as all good lawmen do, parked his car in Marne's driveway and got out. He walked across the road and began to look around.

"Got to be a shell casing or something here," he said to himself. "Every criminal leaves a trace of his presence. Every criminal. They all make a mistake. All of them."

Sheriff Portis walked around the area that was always presumed to have been the shooter's nest, brushing the weeds and grass aside with his boots, pushing sticks and small branches back and forth, back and forth. He pushed a small log aside with his toe and as he was just about to walk back to his car something caught his eye. Something glimmering in the afternoon sun.

A shell casing.

He reached into his pocket and pulled out his gloves used for handling evidence. He put them on and reached down to pick it up. It was a .30-.30 shell. Empty. Was this it? Was this the casing from which the fatal bullet was fired? Yes, it was. It had to be. Who else but the killer would have shot a high powered rifle on the side of the road right across from a house?

The sheriff excitedly put the bullet in an evidence bag, sealed it shut and looked around for more evidence and clues. Finding nothing else he walked back to his car with a spring in his step and hurriedly drove back to the sheriff's department. Once there he immediately summoned his evidence clerk.

"I've got something here, Clarence. I recovered it from the Petakis murder scene, an empty .30-.30 shell. I want it dusted for fingerprints and the results checked against Richard Ambrose. He got a weapons carry permit last year so we should have his fingerprints on file. Do you still know that guy at the FBI who does fingerprints?"

"Yes. I talk to him from time to time."

"Can you see if he can squeeze this in and check for a match?"

"Will do, sir."

"And I want this kept quiet for now."

"Yes, sir," replied Deputy Clarence Hopkins, who rushed back to the evidence lab and began dusting the empty shell, then sent the prints he extracted to his old friend in the FBI fingerprint section.

THE SECOND SATURDAY in December found the sheriff and his family at John's River Farms perusing through the fields of Christmas trees. It had become somewhat of a Portis family tradition to take a day off after Thanksgiving and pick out a nice Blue Ice or cedar, something that would keep its scent throughout the holiday. They found one that they all agreed would be perfect and fit just right in their living room, so the sheriff took out the saw the farm had provided and took it down.

"Yes, this'll do just fine," he said proudly. They dragged it back to their car, turned in the tag from the limb, paid and left. Just as they were turning out onto the road his cell phone rang.

"Hello."

"Sheriff, this is Hopkins. I got those fingerprints results from my friend at the FBI. They came in late last night and I just now saw them."

"Okay, great. What've we got?"

"One hundred percent match for Richard Ambrose."

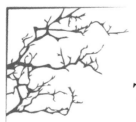

The Arrest

Sheriff Portis went straight to the sheriff's department after erecting the family's Christmas tree, leaving it up to his children to decorate, which he didn't want to do anyway. He called Deputy Hopkins the minute he walked in the door with instructions to bring the fingerprint analysis results to his office.

"This is it, sheriff. The analysis says it's a one hundred percent match. The thumb and index finger were the only ones on the shell casing, but they were enough, in fact plenty. I had my friend check it twice before sending me the results, just to make sure. I'm aware that Ambrose is the clerk's husband so I know how important it is to you that this be as concrete as humanly possible."

"That's an understatement, Clarence. We've got a hot potato on our hands with this one, that's for sure. We can't be anything less than positive before we start swearing out warrants and making arrests."

"Do you want me to get one of the investigators for you?"

"No, I'll handle this one myself. I've got to get a hold of one of the superior court judges. I don't dare approach the magistrate with this. She and Louise are way too close friends for that."

MURDER IN MONTICELLO

The sheriff dialed the number of Judge Milton, the only superior court judge whose office was in Monticello, the others scattered out over four of the seven other counties of the Ocmulgee Judicial Circuit. The phone was answered by the pleasant voice of his secretary, Marie.

"Judge Milton's office."

"Hey, Marie, it's Dave Portis."

"Sheriff, how have you been?"

"Doing well, thanks. And you?"

"Doing just fine, thank you, sheriff. How can I help you today?"

"Is the judge in?"

"He is. Hold on, I'll put you through."

"Henry Milton."

"Hey, judge, it's Sheriff Portis."

"How're you, sheriff?"

"Just fine, thanks. Judge, I have a matter that involves someone of substance in the county and I'd like to come by and discuss it with you, if you have time."

"Oh? Sounds intriguing. You can come by now if you like."

Judge Milton cleared away some files he had put in one of the chairs in front of his desk to make room for the sheriff's visit. A very mild-mannered and well-liked man in his 50s, Henry Milton was always warm and charming to anyone who came before him, never losing his temper with those whom he had to pass judgment on. He had always said that they were nervous enough without him making things worse. He had worked in the District Attorney's Office for years, then elected District Attorney for a short time before running for superior court judge unopposed. Since his first election he had had no opposition and most said it wouldn't have made any difference if he had.

The sheriff arrived at the courthouse and went into the judge's chambers, shutting the door behind him.

"Judge, this is a bit tenuous to say the least, but it's about Marne Petakis' murder."

"Oh, yes, horrible thing. I know she was a controversial figure to say the least, but to have been gunned down like that. Terrible."

"I know," replied the sheriff, thinking that the term "controversial figure" was about the harshest thing Henry Milton ever said about anyone.

"Well, in the course of my investigation I found some letters in her office desk drawer to and from Richard Ambrose, Louise's husband. Some are from him to her and some vice versa. It appears that they were having quite a chess match going on between them about him allegedly violating environmental rules. I interviewed him and he denies not only the allegations, but also that those letters are even genuine. He says he's never even seen them, much less sent or received them.

"Louise was the one who got all this started. She told me that Rick mentioned something about the arguments going back and forth between him and Marne. She said that it seemed really coincidental that Rick and Marne had this going on, and then she turns up murdered.

"She also pointed out that he has several deer rifles, among them a .30-.30. So I went back to the crime scene and this time found a spent .30-.30 shell at the spot where we think the kill shot came from that we had somehow missed earlier. I had it dusted and lo and behold, they're Rick's fingerprints. No doubt

MURDER IN MONTICELLO 139

about it. A one hundred percent match. So I'd like to request an arrest warrant for Rick and a search warrant for his home. I need to get his rifle."

"My God, Dave," said Judge Milton. "You really think the clerk's husband killed Marne Petakis?"

"The puzzle pieces sure do fit together so far, judge. And Louise was a basket case when she came to see me, terrified that Rick was going to do something to her. She seems to have more than a little suspicion that Rick killed Marne. So with everything I've got, I'm here to ask you for an arrest warrant for him."

"Well, this certainly is one fantastic turn of events. Okay, sheriff, you write out the warrants and supporting affidavits and I'll grant them."

"Thank you, Judge Milton."

The sheriff returned to his office and prepared the necessary papers for the arrest of the husband of one of the highest-ranking members of the local court system and the search warrant for his home, especially to retrieve his rifle that all indications were used in the murder of Marne Petakis. The sheriff paused at his computer several times as he pondered the gravity of the situation.

THAT EVENING SHERIFF Portis pulled up at the Ambrose residence with a deputy pulling in behind him. He had no reason to think that Rick would go off the deep end, but he didn't want to take any chances by not following protocol. He knocked on the door and Louise answered.

"Hi, sheriff. Please come in. What can I do for you?"

"Is Rick here, Louise?"

"He's out back in his shop," she answered as she saw the folded-up papers he had in his hand. "Is everything all right?" She silently prayed that this was the moment she had been waiting for.

"Thank you, yes, everything's okay. I just need to see Rick for a minute."

Louise pointed out the back patio door towards the small shop with the lights on inside, where the sheriff and the deputy went to find Rick working on some woodworking project. Rick turned around to see them walk in the door.

"Hey, sheriff, deputy. How's it going?"

"Oh, not so good, Rick. I'm sorry to inform you that you're under arrest for the murder of Marne Petakis. Please turn around and place your hands behind your back. Thank you. You have the right to remain silent, anything you say . . ."

Here Rick went completely deaf to the sheriff's words. What in the world was he hearing? What was he being accused of? How could the sheriff even think that he would murder anyone? What evidence did they possibly have to give them that impression?

"Rick, I also have a search warrant here for your home. I'll need access to your gun cabinet so if it's locked, please give me the key so I don't have to tear it up getting inside."

Rick gave the sheriff the key and was then placed in the back of the deputy's patrol car while Louise watched from the front door steps, weeping the same fake tears she had shed when she talked to the sheriff earlier. She hugged her children and consoled them, telling them that there must be some mistake, that daddy hadn't done anything wrong, all the while feeling a sense of great relief that the plan concocted by her and Cassie was starting out perfectly.

But Rick was only the accused at this point. He would have to be tried, go through the system with all its imperfections, and be convicted. But if tonight was any indication he was well on his way to being out of her life while at the same time hopefully ending the sheriff's scrutiny of her and her friends' embezzlements.

The deputy took Rick to the sheriff's department for booking while the sheriff went into the gun cabinet, took the .30-.30 rifle, and then went through Rick's desk where he kept up with his paperwork.

Rick wasted no time in making his phone call from the jail to his wife.

"Hello."

"Louise, I swear I didn't do anything. I have no idea what they're accusing me of. I mean, I know it's the murder of Marne Petakis, but I don't know what in the world they're talking about. I didn't kill anybody."

"Rick, I know that, honey. I'll get you a lawyer, the best I can find."

"Can you get Royceland Kane?"

"He's awfully expensive, dear, so I doubt it. But let me see what I can do."

"The other day the sheriff asked me to come in and talk with him. He showed me a bunch of letters between Marne and me arguing back and forth about some environmental shit, but I didn't write the ones that are supposed to be from me and I never got the ones that are supposed to be from her. I guess they think that since he found these supposed letters I had a motive for killing Marne. I'm telling you, Louise, this whole goddamn thing is crazy!"

"Just calm down, honey, and keep your wits about you. I'm sure we'll get to the bottom of all this and you'll be all right."

"Well, I sure hope so, Louise. But right now I feel like the whole world has caved in on me."

SHERIFF PORTIS RETURNED to the department and brought Rick's rifle to his office. He called his chief investigator, Paul Wallers, and told him that he needed to have the rifle checked to determine if it had been fired recently, or at least whether the barrel had been cleaned since its last firing.

"I'll do the standard test, sheriff, and let you know."

Later that night the sheriff received a call from Investigator Wallers.

"Hello."

"Sheriff, Waller. I did the test and there is gunpowder residue in the barrel. Unfortunately, I can't really tell you when it was last fired, but I can tell you that the barrel of this gun hasn't been cleaned since the last time it was fired."

"Good work, Paul."

"Thank you, sir. Will there be anything else?"

"Just put it in the evidence room with the Marne Petakis evidence."

"Yes, sir."

THE NEXT DAY LOUISE went to the courthouse but stopped by Cassie's office first, who was just hanging up her coat.

"I take it you've heard?"

"Heard what?"

"Dave arrested Rick last night. He's in the jail right now, charged with murder."

"So it worked. Nice job, Louise. And I take credit for my part in it too."

"Yes, but let's not get ahead of ourselves. He's a long ways from being convicted. A lot can happen between now and then, as you know."

"Yeah, I know. But at least the wheels are rolling. What does he want to do about an attorney?"

"He wants me to get Royce."

"Oooh, he's pretty pricey. Maybe he'd be willing to make you a deal or something. That is, if you want him."

"No, I don't want him. Don't you get it? We want him to be convicted, not acquitted. If Royce represents him he's got a much better chance of getting out of this. Remember, Cassie, the whole idea was to get Portis out of our hair and a fringe benefit will be getting rid of Rick. You don't want him anymore and I sure as hell don't want him. You and I are two women scorned here."

"Yeah, ain't that the truth? Well, see who he wants to hire. Maybe it'll be somebody who's affordable and has never tried a murder case before."

"I'll start asking around. When he hears what their fees are going to be he'll probably tell me to get some hungry kid straight out of law school. Then you and I will have a much better chance of coming out of this with our desired results when it's all over."

SHERIFF PORTIS WALKED back to the inmates' cell area and stood looking at Rick.

"Rick, I'm sorry about all this. I wish with all my heart that this hadn't happened but I've found some things that point straight to you. Do you want to talk about them?"

"There's nothing I would love more, sheriff."

The sheriff then instructed the deputy to unlock Rick's door. Rick sheepishly walked out into the corridor and the deputy told him to turn around and place his hands behind his back as he got out his handcuffs.

"That won't be necessary, deputy," said the sheriff. "Will it, Rick?"

"Oh, the last thing on my mind is doing anything that makes this situation worse, Dave."

The deputy was dismissed and the sheriff walked to his office with Rick beside him. He offered Rick and seat and asked him if he needed anything.

"A cup of that cold water over there would be great, sheriff. Thanks," said Rick as he pointed to the big, plastic water cooler that makes the familiar "blurb, blurb" as you drain it into the cup. The sheriff handed Rick the water and sat down behind his desk.

"Rick, first of all, you know that you don't have to talk to me about all this. You have the right to not incriminate yourself, meaning that you don't have to say anything that could come back and hurt you later. All you have to do is say that you don't want to meet with me like this and I'll send you back to your cell with no hard feelings."

"I don't have a thing to hide, sheriff. Let's talk."

"Well, Okay. Rick, as I showed you before I've got those letters between you and Marne."

"I told you I've never sent nor received any letters from her."

"Okay, Rick, fair enough. *Purported* letters between you and her. And if that was all I had to go on then I wouldn't have arrested you. But when I went back across the road to what we believe is the shooter's nest I found a .30-.30 shell on the ground. I had it dusted for fingerprints. The prints match you, Rick. Match you exactly."

"What?! I haven't shot any guns anywhere near her house! How could that be? How could that possibly be?!"

"I think you know where I'm headed with this Rick. I believe that you holed up over there, maybe parked your car there, waited for her to come home and ambushed her. You ejected the spent shell and I found it with your fingerprints all over it. That's a pretty damaging piece of evidence, Rick, wouldn't you say?"

"Sheriff, if my fingerprints were actually on it then I would agree with you. But it can't possibly have my fingerprints on it. It just can't."

"Well, it does, Rick. It does."

Rick shook his head in amazement as the events of the past day swirled in his mind and he began to sweat.

"Let me ask you this – when was the last time that gun was fired?"

"Last year during hunting season."

"Did you clean it afterwards?"

"Of course, sheriff. I always clean my guns after firing them."

"Do you run the ramrod down the barrel with patches soaked in gun oil?"

"Yes, absolutely. So if you check the barrel it should show that it hasn't been fired in a long time and that the barrel is clean as a whistle."

Sheriff Portis looked down as his desk and back at Rick. "Rick, I just had it tested for gunpowder residue. That gun has been fired since it was last cleaned."

"That's impossible, sheriff! Absolutely impossible! No one fires that gun but me and I know damn well I cleaned it thoroughly after hunting season ended last year!"

"You know, it would help if you were completely honest with me. I know you lied about one thing already."

"Lied about what?"

"Where you were at the time of the murder. You gave me some lame story about going back out at nine or ten ten o'clock at night to make sure some grass seeds hadn't blown off somebody's yard or something, first telling me that it was down

MURDER IN MONTICELLO

near Hillsboro then changing your mind and telling me it was up around Mansfield."

Rick began to really sweat now. What could he say? As it was he stood a good chance of being acquitted, at least in his mind, and returning to his wife afterwards. But if he came clean and told the sheriff that he was in bed with the chief magistrate judge when the murder was committed, he could kiss that good-bye. But at the same time he had intended to file for divorce anyway, so what harm could it do to tell the sheriff the truth? But then that would involve the woman he wanted to be with after the divorce, and if he dragged her into the middle of this that relationship would be over too. He decided to keep his cards close to his vest for now.

"Well, all I can tell you is that I was at a job site to make sure that some grass seeds were secure, sheriff. That's all I can say."

"I don't suppose you have an address for the house, or at least a description and location of it?"

"No, I don't. And I think I'll take you up on your offer to not discuss this right now, sheriff."

Sheriff Portis stood, called in the deputy who was waiting just outside the door, and instructed him to return Rick to his cell.

Kirk Hadley

Louise spent the next several days feigning her worry over her husband with her employees and other courthouse friends as she became more and more the talk of the town. She felt that she had done a good job of making everyone she talked to think that this whole entire event was devastating to her and her family, all the while relishing in the arrest of that damn cheater and liar. She looked on the State Bar website for lawyers who had just joined the Bar, hoping to find someone who would be so inexperienced that Rick wouldn't stand much of a chance. She made some phone calls and was quoted fees ranging from $5,000 to $50,000, so she decided to hire the cheapest one, who also turned out to be the youngest and least experienced one on her list. She had just hung up the phone when she heard a knock.

"Yes? Come in."

"Hi, Louise," said Royceland Kane. "Listen, Louise, I heard about what happened and I can't tell you how sorry I am for you and your children. And Rick. My God, whoever would've thought that he could even be suspected of something like that?"

"Well, I tell you, Royce, I sure hope he can be exonerated at trial. This whole thing has really taken a toll on all of us."

"I'm sure it has. Have you hired an attorney for him yet?

"I think I've got somebody on board, yes. He's a new guy who just set up practice in Covington. He's young, but he went to John Marshall Law School and he's really enthusiastic and seems to be genuinely interested in taking the case."

"Oh, okay. Well, good. I hope it works out for y'all. Anyway, I just wanted to let you know that if there's anything I can do all you need do is ask."

Louise pointedly avoided the subject of Royce representing Rick. A top-notch, experienced attorney who had won as many cases as he had was the last thing she wanted. No, this guy from Covington, straight out of law school who had never tried a felony in his life would do just fine.

"I appreciate that, Royce. Right now all I can ask you to do is pray for us all."

"Consider it done, Louise. Good luck."

Royce then left her office and shut the door behind him. She picked up the phone and called Cassie.

"Magistrate Office."

"I think I've got a lawyer for Rick. Some new kid in Covington named Kirk Hadley. Just joined the Bar and hasn't tried a felony in his life. I asked the clerk up there if she knew anything about him and she said that he tried a DUI case earlier this year and got a hung jury. I think he's the one. And he's very affordable. Have you heard anything else from the sheriff about your fines and all?"

"Not a word."

"Me neither. Looks like it's working so far."

"Indeed it does."

"So what about this video that Marne supposedly took?

"Not a word about that either, Louise. I'm figuring it's one of three things – either she never made a video, or if she did she didn't record it on her phone, or if it was on her phone the sheriff never saw it."

KIRK HADLEY EAGERLY opened his office mail and found a check from Louise for $5,000. He clutched it to his chest and looked up. "Oh, thank you, God. Now I can get my car payment caught up!" He grabbed his dress coat and headed for the door, placing the "closed" sign on it since he had no secretary to tend to the small, low-rent office while he was out. He arrived at the Jasper County Sheriff's Department and went to the window.

"Could I help you, sir?"

"Yes, I'd like an attorney visit with Rick Ambrose, please."

Rick was brought to the attorney visitation room with Hadley on the other side separated by glass.

"Mr. Ambrose?"

"Yes, sir."

"Hi, I'm Kirk Hadley, attorney. Your wife has retained me to represent you. How are you?"

Rick was a little taken at the youthful appearance of this man in whose hands his future, indeed his life depended.

"I see. I'm fine, thank you, Mr. Hadley. Nice to meet you. May I ask how long you've been in practice?"

"Almost a year now, Mr. Ambrose. But believe me I am well versed in criminal law and I intend to represent you to the best of my ability. I've already talked to the assistant district attorney and he gave me some information about your case, so I've got a good idea of what they've got. Now, let's talk about what happened. Tell me, Mr. Ambrose, do you own a .30-.30 rifle?"

"I do, as well as several other hunting rifles."

"When was the last time you shot that particular rifle?"

"It would have been last year during hunting season. I had intended to sight it in for this season but I just hadn't gotten around to it yet."

"What about your fingerprints on the empty shell that was found at the crime scene? Do you have any idea about how that could have happened?"

"Frankly, Mr. Hadley, I have no idea how any of this could have happened. I wasn't there, I haven't shot my rifle since last year, and I sure as hell didn't kill Marne Petakis or anybody else."

"The sheriff says that gunpowder residue was found in the barrel of the gun, indicating that it was fired since it was last cleaned."

"I know, but I swear to you that I haven't fired that gun since last year during hunting season and even then, I cleaned it inside and out afterwards."

"What about these letters between you and Marne Petakis?"

"I'm afraid I don't know anything about those either, Mr. Hadley. I never sent her any letters and never received any from her."

"Well, Mr. Ambrose, that's a problem in that the sheriff has both the shell and the letters. That's going to be a pretty big hurdle to overcome, to be honest. What about your location at the time of the murder? Were you at home?"

Rick looked down at the countertop in his holding room.

"No, I wasn't, Mr. Hadley. That's the problem. I was at a job site and no one else was with me."

"What job site? Where?"

"At a house in Hills, uh, Mansfield. It's a new house and I had been putting down grass seed in the yard. It was windy and the weatherman predicted rain so I wanted to make sure that the hay and straw didn't blow away and expose the seeds before the rain could start."

"And no one was with you there?"

"No, I was alone. It was pretty late at night and since it was a job I could do by myself I didn't want to get any of my employees out there at such an hour."

"Can you tell me exactly which house it is? Does it have a street address or was it too new at the time?"

"I don't think it had a street number assigned to it at the time."

"Really? That's odd. They usually assign a street number to any new house early on, sometimes before it's even built."

"Well, this one didn't have one, Mr. Hadley!" snapped Rick. The pressure of making up an alibi on top of everything else was beginning to cause him to become cantankerous, even with his own lawyer.

"Okay, Mr. Ambrose. I get how much this whole situation must be grinding on you, but you and I have to stick together. Please remember that I'm on your side, okay?"

"I'm sorry, Mr. Hadley. It's just that you're right, I am about at wit's end with this whole damned thing. Say, what about a bond? Think you can get me one?"

"I understand that in this circuit getting a bond for murder is very hard to do, but I'll look into it. Let me see when I can get us a hearing date. Is there anything else you want to tell me or ask me?"

"No, Mr. Hadley, I don't think so. I really appreciate you taking the case and coming by here. Please keep me updated about the bond situation, okay?"

"Will do. Nice to meet you, sir."

"Thanks. You too."

THE JUDGE CALLED THE superior court calendar in his usual manner, going down through the names and asking the opposing attorneys for their announcements.

"Next case, State v. Richard Ambrose, bond hearing. Mr. Clinton and Mr. Hadley. Announcements?"

"Thank you, Your Honor," said Mr. Clinton. "This is a bond motion filed by Mr. Hadley. The state is ready."

"Thank you, Mr. Clinton. Mr. Hadley?"

"Yes, Your Honor, I represent Mr. Ambrose and we're ready."

The judge then looked to the deputy at the holding room door and instructed him to bring Rick out for his bond hearing. Rick took a seat at the counsel table beside Mr. Hadley and Mr. Clinton sat down at his table with the sheriff seated next to him.

"This is the defendant's motion so Mr. Hadley, go ahead."

"May it please the court, I am asking for a bond on behalf of Mr. Ambrose. He's a well-known citizen of the county and I believe we all know that he is the husband of the clerk of court. There is no reason to anticipate that he would be a flight risk or a threat to intimidate witnesses, nor commit felonies while out on bond. He has no criminal history and I believe he is a prime candidate for bond, and I ask the court to set a reasonable bond for Mr. Ambrose."

"Thank you, Mr. Hadley. Mr. Clinton?"

"Your Honor, as you know it is the long-standing practice in our circuit to take the issue of bond in a murder case very cautiously. I concede that Mr. Ambrose has no criminal history and his wife is our clerk of court, but I must oppose bond based on the heinous nature of the crime for which Mr. Ambrose stands accused and for which there is ample evidence that he committed. The victim, Ms. Marne Petakis, had her head literally blown in two by a high-powered rifle that caused her to lose an eyeball and her teeth to bite off her tongue from the impact of the blast. She died instantly and was left lying in her own driveway.

"The Sheriff, who is here to testify should the court desire, found some very incriminating letters in Ms. Petakis' office desk drawer between Mr. Ambrose and Ms. Petakis wherein she was complaining about Mr. Ambrose's job sites and alleged environmental violations she thought he was committing. And the most damning evidence is an empty shell from a .30-.30 rifle found at the shooter's nest that was dusted for fingerprints, which fingerprints match Mr. Ambrose's fingerprints. As you recall, Your Honor granted a search warrant for Mr. Ambrose's house and we recovered a .30-.30 rifle from his gun cabinet. So we believe that we have a pretty air-tight case against Mr. Ambrose and his release on bond would cause me concern that he would be a flight risk. Thank you, Your Honor."

"Thank you, Mr. Clinton.."

The judge wasted no time in making a ruling.

"I find that the defendant is a flight risk and I deny bond."

THE NEXT DAYS, WEEKS and months passed slowly for Rick sitting in the Jasper County Jail. He regularly saw his attorney, Kirk Hadley, and became more and more convinced that Mr. Hadley was far too inexperienced to represent him in a murder case, much less win it. He couldn't understand why Louise had put such a great deal of stock in Mr. Hadley, seeking him out and hiring him without even telling Rick that she had done so.

His case came up on two criminal trial calendars, each time being continued in favor of trying older cases. Finally, after he had been in jail for eight months, it came up for the third time. Rick remained in the holding room adjacent to the courtroom, listening intently for his name.

"Next case, Your Honor, is State v. Richard Ambrose, number 14 on the calendar," said Jamie Clinton. "The state announces 'ready for trial.'"

Kirk Hadley stood and said, "The defense announces ready as well, judge."

"Be here Monday morning to begin the trial," instructed the judge.

The attorneys told the judge that they would be ready and left the courtroom to work over the weekend putting the finishing touches on the case.

Mr. Hadley went by the jail before returning to his office in Covington. This time he and Rick met in a room together, face to face, with no glass separating them. Rick had been a very well-behaved inmate since his incarceration there so the sheriff felt that he had earned the right to this more direct meeting with his lawyer.

"Rick, we're up Monday morning. I wanted to talk to you one more time about your alibi."

"Okay," said Rick, dreading the subject of the alibi. He knew that he was in bed with the magistrate judge at the time of the murder and what ramifications would befall him should he disclose that.

"You say you were at a new house under construction up near Mansfield, right? How far from the Newton County line?"

"Oh, I don't know, Mr. Hadley. Maybe a mile or so, maybe less."

"Was it a two-story house, flat, duplex, what?"

"I didn't pay much attention to the house itself. I was interested in the yard."

"I realize that, but you must've noticed it. I'm trying to identify which one it is so I can at least take a picture of it to show to the jury."

Rick tried to steer the conversation away from the subject of an alibi.

"Well, if you can't find the exact house, what else have we got in the way of a defense?"

"I must admit, not much. The state can get the letters found in Ms. Petakis' house into evidence and the bullet shell they found at the murder scene. You still have no idea how your fingerprints got onto that shell?"

"None whatsoever. It's almost like they were put there purposely by somebody trying to frame me or something."

"Now, Rick, that's crazy. No one is trying to frame you. Who in the world would have the least motive for doing that?"

"Yeah, I guess you're right. I suppose I'm just pulling at straws at this point."

"So it looks like we're on for Monday?"

"Yes."

"Thank you, Mr. Hadley. See you then."

"Fingers crossed, Mr. Ambrose."

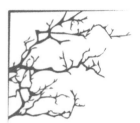

The Trial

The next Monday Mr. Hadley and Rick sat in the courtroom, Mr. Hadley with his nicest suit and Rick with some nice clothes brought to him by Louise. He had to be viewed as innocent until proven guilty so he had to have on street clothes instead of the jail suit. Knowing that he was in custody would do what lawyers call "prejudice the jury". Rick sat quietly and noticed Mr. Hadley fidgeting.

"I call the case of State v. Ambrose. Gentlemen?"

"The state announces ready for trial, Your Honor," said Mr. Clinton.

Mr. Hadley felt a lump in his throat as his chest heaved. He slowly stood up and said, "Ready for trial."

"Very well," said Judge Milton."

The judge then turned to the jury and began his usual colloquy, instructions for what to expect for the trial, an outline of the procedures they would see in the next couple of days or so, the role of the various people involved, and so forth. Rick sat there with a bead of sweat on his forehead not unlike his mistress when she was presiding in court or was being questioned by the sheriff about her fines. Jury selection took most of the morning and went into the early afternoon, resulting in the twelve people seated only a few feet away from

Rick who would decide his fate for the rest of his life. He said a silent prayer as he thought about the gravity of the situation.

Then came the opening statements by the attorneys. Jamie Clinton handed Danyale some papers, stood up, adjusted his suit coat, nodded to the judge and opposing counsel and turned to the jury. His demeanor was that of a seasoned and experienced attorney and his delivery was eloquent and matched his appearance. He stood before the jurors and began talking, no notes in hand.

"Ladies and gentlemen of the jury. Good morning. As stated earlier, I'm Jamie Clinton, district attorney for the Ocmulgee Judicial Circuit.

"The evidence will show that Mr. Ambrose, the gentleman seated at counsel table there, had every reason to see Ms. Petakis dead. He had what we in the law call 'MOM', motive, opportunity and means.

"His motive? Well, you will see letters that went back and forth between the defendant and his victim wherein she accused him of various environmental violations. He reacted to her letters with equal venom, telling her at one point that she wasn't worth responding to. Clearly, he had a motive.

"His opportunity? On a cloudy night on the Monday before Thanksgiving last year he drove to her secluded residence and crouched in the bushes just across the street waiting for her to come home. When she drove up, got out of her car and walked to her mailbox he saw his opportunity. Yes, that's when he committed this heinous crime.

"And his method, Oh, yes, ladies and gentlemen, his method. His method was to aim his .30-.30 deer rifle, a high-powered weapon at her head and split it in two with one shot. So how do we know he fired the fatal blow? The empty shell casing found at the scene with his fingerprints on it betray him.

"That's right, ladies and gentlemen, the bullet he fired was his own, the gun retrieved from his home was his own, the reason for killing her was his own. Indeed, this murder was his own."

With that Mr. Clinton sat down and yielded to the young Kirk Hadley. He stood, pulled up his pants slightly, took a drink of water from the styrofoam cup on his table and sat it back down, catching the edge of his file on the bottom and spilling it on top of the table. Rick pulled back to keep from getting soaked as Mr. Hadley nervously reached for some paper towels and began sopping it up. Clearly embarrassed, he turned around to the jury and smiled.

"Well, doing that wasn't in my notes."

There was a slight chuckle from the jurors at Mr. Hadley's attempt at levity which did little to put his mind at ease or make him less nervous. But to his credit he regained his composure and after fumbling with his written notes began to speak.

"Ladies and gentlemen, I am Kirk Hadley, Mr. Ambrose's attorney. I must begin by taking issue with Mr. Clinton's allegation that Mr. Ambrose had any motive for killing Marne Petakis. The truth is, ladies and gentlemen, that he never sent nor received the letters the state intends to introduce into evidence and that Mr. Clinton referred to in his opening statement. In fact, Mr. Ambrose didn't even know Marne Petakis. Oh, like most in this county he knew who she was. Her name was constantly in the local newspaper and on social media complaining about this and that. So sure, he was familiar with who she was, but he did not know her nor did he have any motive at all for murdering her.

"I submit that when this trial is over you will agree that Mr. Ambrose should be found 'not guilty'. Thank you."

"Call your first witness," instructed Judge Milton.

Sheriff Portis took the witness stand. He had a calmness about him that was rare for witnesses during trials. His likable personality would be well-received by the jury and Mr. Clinton was glad that he had decided to open with him as his first witness.

"Sheriff, I want to take you to the day of Ms. Petakis' murder. Where were you when it happened?"

"In Louisiana visiting relatives. I always like to be here during the Thanksgiving holiday, so my family and I went out of state the week before with the intention of returning on Wednesday, the day before Thanksgiving. But when my chief deputy called me and told me what had happened I decided to catch an earlier flight and come home early. I arrived in town and got to the crime scene at around two o'clock in the afternoon on Tuesday, the day after the murder, which was around ten o'clock at night on Monday."

"Did you have occasion to visit the crime scene again after you had initially left it?"

"Yes, I did, several days later. It had occurred to me that we might have failed to find the empty bullet casing, the empty shell as it's called. So I went back there to take a second look."

"Is that unusual, sheriff, for something to be missed when searching a crime scene, especially something as small as a shell casing?"

"Oh, by no means, Mr. Clinton. In fact, I would say it would be more unusual for law enforcement to find everything the very first time. There's a lot of debris, sticks, grass, limbs, you name it on the side of the road over there. So I wanted to walk it one more time and take a much closer look than we had before. I pushed back some sticks and other debris with my boots and sure enough, I found a shell casing."

"That would be Exhibit '1' here, sheriff. Please take a look at this and let me know what that is."

"It's the bullet casing I found at the crime scene. It's from a .30-.30 rifle. We dusted it for fingerprints and got a match."

"And whose fingerprints are on this bullet shell, sheriff?"

"Richard Wayne Ambrose, the gentleman seated at counsel table."

"And did you then conduct a search of Mr. Ambrose's home?"

"Yes, I was granted and executed a search warrant and found a Marlin .30-.30 rifle that shoots this very bullet."

"Objection, Your Honor," said Mr. Hadley as he popped to his feet. "The witness is drawing a conclusion by stating that Mr. Ambrose's gun fired that very bullet."

"Sustained," responded Judge Milton. "Sheriff, did you mean that his particular gun fired that particular bullet, or that his gun fires that type of bullet?"

"Poor wording on my part, judge. I meant that his rifle is a .30-.30 caliber and fires a .30-.30 bullet, the kind we have here. I didn't mean to imply that his rifle definitely fired this bullet."

"So," continued Mr. Clinton, "it is your testimony that it is the same type of weapon that fires that type of bullet, correct?"

"Correct."

"Did you conduct any type of test to determine whether the gun had been fired since it was last cleaned?"

"I did. It's called a gunpowder residue test and the results indicated the presence of gunpowder residue in the barrel, meaning that the gun has not been cleaned since its last firing."

"Thank you. Now, sheriff, did you interview Mr. Ambrose at any point during your investigation?"

"Yes, I did."

"Did you ask him about his fingerprints on the bullet?"

"I did. He said that he had no idea how they got on there."

"Did you ask him about the gunpowder residue in the gun barrel?"

"Yes, and he said that he hasn't fired the gun since it was cleaned at the close of hunting season last year."

"Now, you said that the murder occurred at around ten o'clock at night on the Monday before Thanksgiving. Did you ask him where he was at the time of the murder?"

"Yes, I did. He said that he was at a job site."

"A job site? What kind of business is he in?"

"He's a lawn care specialist, Mr. Clinton. He said that he had worked on a client's yard and had put down some grass seed and covered it with hay and straw. I asked him why he went back to the job site at such an hour and he said that he wanted to make sure that the seeds didn't scatter in the wind and wash away since it was forecast to rain that night."

"Were you able to corroborate his alibi?"

"I'm afraid not. He didn't have any of his employees with him there and he wasn't able to provide the names of any witnesses who could substantiate his story that he was there at the time of the murder. And he gave no definite description or address of the house where he was working on the lawn."

"Thank you. Now, I'd like to turn your attention to these letters, Exhibit '2'. Please tell the jury how they came to be in your possession."

"I conducted a search of the house where Ms. Petakis lived and worked in a home office and found some letters in her desk drawer."

"Are these the letters you found, sheriff?" asked Mr. Clinton.

"They are."

"Sheriff, I'd like you to read these letters to the jury."

The courtroom sat silent listening to the letters read one by one to the jury, letters whose content had been previously undisclosed to the public. Rick scanned the jurors' faces as they heard the sheriff's words, occasionally looking at him with a disdained look. When Sheriff Portis finished he laid the letters down on the witness stand and took a drink of water. Mr. Clinton was quiet for that infinitesimal period of time that though short seems to last for hours and has the effect of saying "well, how about that?"

"Your witness, Mr. Hadley."

Mr. Hadley stood up and made his way to the podium. "Sheriff, you say that Mr. Ambrose owns a .30-30 rifle?"

"Yes."

"And this is deer country down here, isn't that right?"

"Yes, it is."

"In fact, Jasper County touts itself as the Deer Capital of Georgia, doesn't it?"

The sheriff smiled. "Yes, we are indeed."

"And a .30-.30 is a deer hunting rifle, a high-powered rifle, isn't it?"

"It is."

"Do you have one yourself, sheriff?"

"As a matter of fact I do."

"As do I," said Mr. Hadley.

"But I don't have any .30-.30 bullets with Mr. Ambrose's fingerprints on them, Mr. Hadley. Except, of course, for that one on the table there."

Mr. Hadley felt deflated after the sheriff's comment that he blamed himself for inviting. Of course it's not the caliber of rifle, or that Jasper County is the Deer Capital of Georgia, or that practically everybody in the county hunts deer, or that so many of them have a .30-.30 rifle. It's the shell, that damnable shell with his fingerprints on it! That's the key to the link between Rick and the murder weapon and the murder. "How stupid could I be?" he thought.

"Just one more question about the fingerprints, sheriff, if I may. Who dusted for the fingerprints?"

"Deputy Clarence Hopkins."

"And who compared the prints found on the shell with Mr. Ambrose to come up with the match?"

"The FBI in Atlanta."

"Was the FBI asked to compare the fingerprints on the shell to all individuals in their system, or did you specifically ask if they matched Mr. Ambrose's fingerprints?"

"We asked them if they matched Mr. Ambrose's fingerprints only."

"So the FBI already had somebody in mind to match those prints to when they were asked to do the comparison."

"Yes."

"So you didn't ask them if the prints matched anybody else in their data base, only Mr. Ambrose?"

"That's correct."

"Well, isn't that a little myopic, sheriff? I mean, you basically pointed to the person you wanted to get a match for. What if they actually would have matched someone else?"

"It's not like a photo lineup, Mr. Hadley, where you have an array of photos of eight or ten people and ask the witness if he recognizes the one who robbed him, for example. This is different."

"So you called them yourself?"

"Well, actually no, Deputy Hopkins did."

"You had a deputy call the FBI to ask for a fingerprint comparison in a murder case? Wouldn't that more properly be done by you or a higher-ranking officer in the department than a deputy?"

"Well, generally yes, but you see, Deputy Hopkins used to be a clerk there and he knew a guy who could get it done much more quickly than going through normal channels."

"Oh, so you pulled a few strings with the FBI to get a fingerprint match between the shell casing and Mr. Ambrose, giving them no other person on earth to compare the fingerprints to than Mr. Ambrose?"

"Well, I wouldn't call it pulling any strings, Mr. Hadley. It was just more of a request to a friend by Deputy Hopkins to get it done quicker."

"So your deputy asked his friend at the FBI to hurry up and run a set of prints to see if they matched those of somebody you already had as a suspect, not the fingerprint data base at large."

"I suppose that's one way of putting it."

"Now, about these alleged letters, sheriff. You say you found them in Ms. Petakis' home office desk drawer?

"That's correct."

"I see that the ones from her are unsigned while the ones that are supposed to be from my client bear his signature."

"That's not unusual, Mr. Hadley. I'm sure you recognize that when you prepare a letter for someone you sign the outgoing one but not necessarily the file copy you keep for your records."

"Did you conduct a search of Mr. Ambrose's home?"

"I did."

"Did you find any of these letters that were supposedly sent to him in his effects?"

"I did not."

"Did you find any of the letters that he is alleged to have sent to her, even unsigned ones as you describe, in his effects?"

"I did not."

"Don't you find that a bit unusual, sheriff, that she was the only one with these letters in her possession? That Mr. Ambrose had nothing remotely resembling these letters in his records?"

"Mr. Hadley, I have no explanation as to why Ms. Petakis still had these letters and Mr. Ambrose did not. There could be a host of reasons that he never kept anything that he received from her."

"Actually, sheriff, isn't it true that you have no evidence at all that he actually *did* receive any of these letters from her?"

"No, I can't say that I do."

"One more question, sheriff. Did you find any of the envelopes that these letters were sent in?"

"No, I didn't."

"Thank you, sheriff. No further questions," said Mr. Hadley as he resumed his seat at his table.

"Re-direct, Mr. Clinton?" asked the judge.

"Yes, sir. Sheriff, do you have any indication that asking for an expedited analysis of the fingerprints did anything to compromise the accuracy of the findings?"

"No, sir."

"Is it the standard operating procedure to ask that fingerprints be compared to a known set of fingerprints for a particular individual that you're interested in rather than a match with the entire fingerprint data base?"

"It is. I can't imagine how long it would take for a fingerprint match to be done where you simply ask them if there's anyone in their date base that matches the prints you have, even with computers. That's why we always ask if they match with the ones we have from a person of interest."

"Thank you."

"It's five minutes until five, so that's enough for today, ladies and gentlemen," said the judge. "We'll reconvene tomorrow morning at 9:00."

Kirk Hadley arrived at the Jasper County Jail after the inmates had been given supper to see Rick. They went into the small room and sat down. Rick had the look of a man who had just completed a triathlon.

"Well, what do you think? How are we looking?"

"It's the same case it was, Rick. The state made some headway with your fingerprints on the shell casing but I was able to challenge it being your .30-.30 that fired it when there are so many of those rifles in this county."

"But the fingerprints were damaging, weren't they?"

"I'm afraid so, Rick. I'm not going to lie to you. Criminal trials are always an uphill battle for the defense, and yours is no exception. If they didn't have any evidence they wouldn't have brought the case in the first place. That's the way it works. It just is."

"So what's tomorrow? Where do you think they'll go?"

"I imagine that they'll get into the particulars about the murder itself tomorrow, Rick. The deputies who were first on the scene, the ambulance attendants, the doctor who pronounced her dead. None of them will do you much damage as far as our defense is concerned since they don't really have anything to say about your involvement. But those photos of her dead body aren't going to help . . . they never do. Sometimes the jury just seeing something like that is prejudicial, but I'm afraid there's nothing I can do about that. The state has a right to show what happened to their victim. Our defense has been and continues to be that we're awfully sorry that this woman got killed, but that you had nothing to do with it. That's where we are."

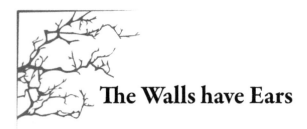

The Walls have Ears

"Ready to go, gentlemen?" asked the judge.

Both attorneys nodded their assent and the judge said to Mr. Clinton, "Call your next witness."

The state, through its district attorney who looked like he just walked out of a Gentlemen's Quarterly magazine, called witness after witness, from ambulance attendants to deputy sheriffs to the emergency room personnel. Mr. Hadley had few or no questions for them since they didn't offer any testimony against his client as the shooter.

The day passed relatively quickly in this major trial for this little town. The jury was shown photos of the body of Marne Petakis, photos of her while alive, close-up photos of the head wound, gut-wrenching and disgusting images that clearly made several members of the jury uneasy.

Court adjourned for the afternoon and everyone was dismissed by Judge Milton with instructions to be back the next morning. The state was wrapping up its case with only the treating physician left to testify. Rick and Kirk met again at the jail after court adjourned as they had done the day before.

"Why do they need the doctor at all, Kirk? I mean, it's obvious that she's dead, whoever killed her."

"Well, I know it seems a little redundant to a layman, Rick, but they have to prove that Marne Petakis was once a live human being and is no longer alive. I expect the doctor to just testify that she died of a single bullet wound to the head. I don't anticipate him pointing the finger at any particular individual as the shooter."

"So how do you think it's going so far?"

"You asked me that yesterday, Rick, and my answer is the same. It's unfolding pretty much as I expected it to. The state's major, very major evidence against you are the letters and the bullet shell. They've linked you to the shell by your fingerprints, although I did make some points on cross-examination. The same with the letters. But who knows? These damn things are a crapshoot at best, to tell you the truth."

"You don't sound very reassuring."

Hadley looked directly at Rick. "I'm not in the reassurance business, Rick. I'm in the legal business. I go by evidence. I don't get excited or discouraged about cases. I'm cold, calculating, and unemotional about my trials. I don't console or dispirit my clients at all, no matter how a trial is going. Doing that wouldn't do my clients or me any good at all. If you want reassurance that everything's gonna be all right, talk to your preacher. The law is a fact-based business and the fact is, Rick, that they've got your fingerprints on the shell casing that they contend fired the bullet that killed the victim and it matches the kind of gun you own. Now, I think I made some headway with my cross examination of the sheriff on the fingerprints being done the way they were, as well as the fact that so many people have that kind of rifle down here. I also challenged the letters and maybe that hit home with some of the jurors too. But the facts are what they are. So prepare yourself for the worst and if the best happens, then that's great."

Rick struggled to digest his attorney's words but the truth was, he was right. His fingerprints, however they got there, were on the shell casing and it was the kind of bullet that goes in his gun. And those letters. Those damn letters. Rick knew that he never sent nor received any such letters between him and Marne. His only interaction with her was a brief, albeit hostile encounter at the door of the local grocery store. Nothing more.

The two finished their meeting, shook hands, and Kirk walked towards the door to leave. He stopped, turned around, and gave Rick a hug.

"I'm doing everything I can, Rick. I hope you realize that."

Rick could hold in his emotions no longer. He began to weep and said, "I know you are, Kirk. And I appreciate it. More than you know. I just know that I didn't kill her and I'm terrified that I'm going to go to prison an innocent man."

"If that happens, Rick, it'll be in spite of us both. Now I want you to think about whether you want to testify or not tomorrow. Remember, only you can make that decision."

RICK TOSSED AND TURNED throughout the night. When he did manage to doze off he woke up suddenly in a cold sweat. His arms ached. His legs ached. His back ached. He was a tormented man, a man unable to get a grasp on what his future held. Would he be acquitted and go back to Louise and the children, resume his lawn business, continue his affair with

Cassie? Would he get divorced? Was Louise already planning on divorcing him regardless of the outcome of the trial?

Or would he be convicted of murder, something he knew he hadn't committed? Would he be sent to Reidsville State Prison, Autry State Prison, Baldwin State Prison in nearby Milledgeville? What would happen to his already unraveling life? He couldn't escape the torment of those questions eating away at his mind.

But strangely enough, one other thought inexplicably came to his mind: What was Cassie doing on Armour Road meeting some guy at daybreak all those months ago? Why such a question came to his mind he could not tell, especially at a time like this. There was no rhyme or reason to its presence in his head. It had nothing to do with him, nothing to do with anything of interest to him. With his own life hanging in the balance, he's thinking about something Cassie did last November? Why should he care about what Cassie did, then or now? What difference could that possibly make to him? Surely, he thought to himself, he had plenty to worry about of his own concern.

But he couldn't shake the notion that her actions that day had something to do with his case. But what? And why?

He turned over one last time to try to get at least some sleep. He tried everything he could – counting sheep, "singing" songs in his head, pretending that he was lying on a boat in the middle of the ocean gently drifting with the swells of the waves.

But why was she on Armour Road?

COURT WAS CONVENED the next morning and shortly after the jurors were all seated, Jamie Clinton's secretary walked up and whispered something in his ear. He made one of those faces that says "oh, no" without saying a word, motioned for Kirk Hadley to join in at the judge's bench, and when they got there he told Judge Milton what he didn't want to hear.

"Your Honor, I'm so sorry, but our witness, Dr. Franklin, is not going to be able to be here today. He's had a family emergency and says it'll be Monday before he can come. I'm so sorry and I'm sure you know this can't be helped. Just one of those things that happens when you have a trial. Can we adjourn until Monday morning, please?"

Judge Milton groaned, turned to the jury and said, "Ladies and gentlemen, I've been given word that one of the witnesses has had some sort of emergency and can't be here today. I apologize for any inconvenience, but these things happen sometimes. You are excused until Monday morning at nine o'clock. Everyone have a nice rest of the week and weekend. Thank you."

The jury left the courtroom and the courtroom personnel soon followed.

"That's just one of those things, huh, Jamie?" said Sheriff Portis to the district attorney. "Well, I guess we've got a day off from this. You know, I think I'll just take the day off myself and go to the pond and do some fishing. It's been a while. You wanna come?"

"You know, Dave, don't mind if I do. Let me run by the house and change clothes and I'll meet you at the department."

"I'll get some bait. See you in an hour or so."

THAT EVENING THE COURTHOUSE staff had left for the day when Louise walked into her office and was followed a few minutes later by Cassie. Louise had been running behind in her usual paperwork most days during the trial, so working into the evening had become somewhat commonplace for her. They had no need to close the door to talk since everyone had left and they were alone.

"Well," began Cassie, "how's the trial going? I can't come up there for long periods of time so I can only get a glimpse from time to time as I pass through. How's it looking?"

"I think Jamie has an air-tight case myself, Cassie. At this point I don't think F. Lee Bailey could get him acquitted."

"Who?"

"Never mind. Anyway, he's as good as convicted, the way I see it. Then as soon as he's sent to prison I'll file for divorce and you and me will both be rid of his sorry ass!"

"Yeah, then we can get back to our, uh, business enterprises. I tell you, Louise, that was the easiest money I ever made in my life. Bilking these hicks out of money is a piece of cake. They'll pay just about anything just to get me off their backs. And I know you've got your hands in a few pies around your own office, too."

"Yeah, that's for sure, Cassie. I don't know what was easier, skimming money from the county or setting Rick up to take the fall for Marne's murder. Both very simple and satisfying. And those letters you thought up, what a genius move. And his fingerprints I got him to put on that bullet shell; I can't help but take credit for a great job on that. A great job by us both. And you getting Harry Blakely to do the shooting, what a move. And Portis hasn't said a word about your fines or anything since all this started. The murder and Rick's arrest took the spotlight right off of us and onto him, just like we planned."

"Yeah, we outdid ourselves, didn't we? He deserves it. He's a prick. I'll be glad to see him in a prison jumpsuit. And to know that we put him there. The crime of the century, at least in this little hamlet."

The two women laughed at their schemes as Louise took a bottle of whiskey out of her desk drawer along with two glasses, poured them full, handed Cassie one and raised her glass. "To us."

"To us," followed Cassie as they then clinked their glasses together, gulped down their spirits, rinsed out their glasses in the private sink in Louise's office and put them back in the desk drawer.

"I came here to catch up on some paperwork but you know what, fuck it. I'm calling it a night, Cassie. Let's go to the Mexican place and celebrate. I know the son of a bitch ain't been convicted yet, but that's just a formality now. Come on, let's go. There's plenty more liquor next door."

The two women walked out of Louise's private office, turned off the lights and closed the door with a bang.

A lone figure walked out from behind a desk she had been crouched behind the whole time, listening intently to the conversation, of which she heard every word. Sarah Hankins set her dust rag and cleaning spray down on top of one of the desks, pondering for a moment what she had just heard.

These two women had framed an innocent man for murder. They were obviously involved in some sort of money skimming operation. She had to do something.

SARAH HANKINS GOT HOME a little after ten o'clock and found Jacob in bed as usual on her late nights from her cleaning jobs. She eased the bedroom door open and found him sound asleep. Debating whether to wake him or not, she decided that it was best to talk to him while the evening's events were still fresh in her mind.

"Jacob?"

"Hmm? Huh? Sarah? What's up? I was asleep."

"I know, and I'm sorry to wake you up. But I heard some things while I was doing my cleaning at the courthouse tonight and I need to tell you about it."

Jacob yawned and sat up in bed, rubbing his eyes. "Why? What did you hear?"

"Well, I was cleaning the clerk's office like I always do on Wednesday nights. I was down on my knees scrubbing some stains on the floor when two women came in, I think the clerk and the magistrate judge. They didn't see or hear me and they went in the clerk's private office but left the door open, I guess because they thought the office was empty. They started talking about how they set up that guy who's on trial up there for murder, faked letters to implicate him, had him put his fingerprints on some bullet or something, and even mentioned that some guy named Blakely actually killed that lady. I swear

I was frozen in fear, Jacob. I was scared to death that they'd see me in there and I might be next!"

"Sarah, are you sure of what you heard? I mean, this is really big! Sounds like something you'd see in a movie."

"Jacob, I'm completely sure."

"You say that damn magistrate judge was one of them? That Manson woman?"

"Yeah, that's her. I've seen her in her office upstairs before. That's the one."

"You know what's funny? Last year, I think it wasn't long before Thanksgiving, she was parked on the road in front of our house yellin' at some guy about a fine or somethin'. It was not long after daybreak. He gave her some money, then they both drove off, then that Marne lady, the one that got killed, walked out of the woods and called somebody on her cell phone to come pick her up. When the car drove up to get her she said that she got it all on video. I figured she was talkin' about the judge and that guy. Then the next thing you know she turns up murdered. Ain't all this weird?"

"It sure is, Jacob. What do you want to do?"

"I think we both need to talk to the sheriff."

JACOB AND SARAH HANKINS arrived at the sheriff's department early the next morning. They went to the receptionist's window and asked to see Sheriff Portis. A few minutes later he walked out into the lobby.

"Hi, I'm Sheriff Portis. May I help you?"

"Hello, sheriff. I'm Jacob Hankins and this is my wife Sarah. We have somethin' we'd both like to discuss with you if you can spare us a little time, please."

"Of course. May I ask what this is about?"

"It's about that guy on trial for murder at the courthouse, sheriff," replied Sarah. "We have some information that might be very important to everybody."

"Well, come on in, by all means."

They went back to the sheriff's private office and shut the door. The sheriff, ever the gentleman, offered them both a seat and a cup of water or coffee. They took the seat and thanked him but politely declined the drinks.

"So, what do you have to tell me?"

The two looked at each other and Sarah told Jacob to go first.

"Sheriff, I live out on Armour Road. Late last year in November a car parked in front of the house and a lady got out. I recognized her as the Judge Manson from the courthouse but she didn't see me. She stood there for a couple of minutes when another car pulled up, stopped, and some guy got out. I don't know who he was. Anyway, they started talkin' and he must've said somethin' she didn't like because she just sort of went off on him, yellin' and carryin' on. She said somethin' to him about payin' her some money like a fine, and he gave her some cash. She got in her car and drove away, kickin' up dust and all. Then I looked up and that Marne lady, the one that got killed, come stumblin' out of the woods with a cell phone in her hand. She called somebody and told them to come pick her up and another car then drove up to get her. She opened the door and right before she got in I heard her say somethin' about gettin' the whole thing on video."

"Mr. Hankins, are you sure it was Judge Manson that you saw?"

"Positive, sheriff. No doubt about that in my mind. And I'm sure it was that Marne who was there a few minutes after she left, too."

"And that ain't the half of it, sheriff," interjected Sarah. "I clean the courthouse at night and last night I was in the clerk's office kneeled down scrubbing the floor when two women came in, I'm pretty sure the clerk and that Manson woman. I saw and heard them but they didn't know I was in there. They went in the clerk's private office but left the door open and I heard them say something about this whole trial being brought against an innocent man, how they made up some letters, how they got him to put his fingerprints on a bullet just so they could frame him. And you know the real kicker – they talked about how they got some guy named Blakely to kill that lady. I was scared to death, sheriff! I was terrified that they might see me in there. But they didn't and they eventually left. I went home and told Jacob and we decided we'd better let you know what was going on."

The sheriff leaned back in his chair and looked up at the ceiling. What in the world was he hearing? Could this all really have happened?

"Tell me, Mr. Hankins, did you see how Marne recorded the conversation between Judge Manson and that man out in front of your house?"

"No, she must've done that from back in the woods a little ways. But she was holdin' up her cell phone when she came out of the woods."

"And you say they talked about a guy named Blakely?"

"Yes, sir," said Sarah. "Said his first name was Henry or something."

"Harry?"

"Yeah, that's it, Harry Blakely."

"I will look into all this immediately, Mr. and Mrs. Hankins. Here's my card. If you think of anything else please let me know."

"We will," said Jacob.

The sheriff thanked them and the Hankins left. He immediately called Justin Petakis, Marne's son.

"Hello."

"Justin? It's Sheriff Portis."

"Hello, sheriff. What can I do for you?"

"Well, I was wondering if I could take a look at your mother's cell phone one more time. There's something I think I might've missed."

"Oh, I'm sorry, sheriff, but it's long gone. I threw that thing away. Too many memories, you know? Every time I looked at it I thought about her, so I printed out her photos and destroyed the phone. Sorry."

The sheriff's heart sank when he heard those words. "Oh, I see. Well, thanks anyway."

"You bet."

Rick's Big Decision

The sheriff pulled into Harry Blakely's yard to find him sitting on a new lawn chair, part of a new set of yard furniture, beer in hand. He got out of his car and raised his hand in a wave. Blakely did not return the gesture.

"Little early in the morning for that, ain't it, Mr. Blakely?"

"I'm on my own property, drinking my own beer, and I ain't behind the wheel of nothin' nor actin' a fool, sheriff. What's your beef?"

"Hey, no beef, Mr. Blakely. I just wanted to know if I could talk to you a minute. Something has come up and if you don't mind I've got a few ques... hey, look at this lawn furniture, will you?! Nice! I'll bet that baby cost you a pretty penny, huh?"

"That's my business."

The sheriff slowed his gait and continued to stand, waiting to see if Mr. Blakely would invite him to sit down. He did not.

"Look, Mr. Blakely, I know you're sore with me and, I guess, all of us on the state's side after your trial last year. But the evidence pointed in your direction so that's the direction we went. It wasn't anything personal, never is. Just following our leads, that's all."

"Well, you came up short on my trial, sheriff, so why don't you just leave me be? Or are you here to arrest me again for some crime I didn't commit?"

"I just wanted to ask you a few questions, Mr. Blakely. Do you know the clerk of court, Ms. Ambrose, or Cassie Manson, the magistrate court judge? Have you ever met either one of them?"

"Well, seeing as how Ms. Ambrose was in court during my whole sham trial sittin' up there like a goddamn queen on her throne you could say that I know who she is, yeah. As for the other chick, who, Castor Massey?"

"Cassie Manson, Mr. Blakely. She's the magistrate judge."

"No, can't say that I know either one of them, sheriff. What else you got for me?"

"I just didn't know whether you'd ever had any contact with either one of them, I mean, outside of court, you know. Like you said, Ms. Ambrose was in the courtroom during your trial."

"Yeah, she was, wasn't she? Like I said, a queen on her throne."

"But you have never seen Judge Manson?"

Don't ring a bell, sheriff."

"Well, OK, I was just checking. I thought maybe she'd been out here before, but I guess that's a pretty foolish presumption, isn't it? I mean, why would she come to your house anyway?"

"Yeah, her fat ass would probably fall right through them rotten porch slats but hey, I'm gettin' some lumber in here next week to fix 'em! Yeah, gonna fix this place up real nice."

"Well, good for you, Mr. Blakely. I'm glad to see things turning around for you. I mean that. You were acquitted by a jury of your peers and that's fair enough. Well, I'll be on my way."

"Suit yourself."

The sheriff opened his car door, held it open and turned back around.

"By the way, how'd you know she's fat?"

Harry Blakely got quiet.

"I didn't say she was."

"No, of course you didn't. Well, thanks for your time, Mr. Blakely. I hope things are going well for you."

Blakely stood and tried his best to be as sarcastic as possible, sounding more like a hick than usual as he tried to imitate a British accent. "So good of you to come by, Mr. High Sheriff, sir. Do drop in again. Perhaps we could have a cup of tea."

Sheriff Portis gritted his teeth at this man's insolence but being a professional, he knew better than to pursue the matter any further. He drove back to his office and got on his computer.

"Hmm," he said to himself as he recognized the lawn furniture style that Blakely had. "The only place that sells that exact same set is that home improvement store in Covington. Think I'll pay them a visit."

He went to his file drawer and pulled out the old Blakely file, took out the mug shot, and left. He arrived at the store in the early afternoon and approached one of the cashiers and asked if she had ever seen the man in the photo before.

"Yeah, I think so," said Molly, the cashier who had sold the furniture to Blakely. "He came by here and bought a nice set of lawn furniture that we carry. It was like this one over here," she said, pointing to an identical set. "Yeah, I remember him. White guy, kinda overweight, reeked of beer to tell you the truth, but boy, what a fistful of money. Paid cash, too, over eleven hundred dollars. But he was a little creepy too, sheriff, you know? I joked with him about waving around that kind of money in public. He said something like 'Well, anybody tries to take this wad from me and I'll kill him like I killed the others.' Kind of freaked me out, to tell you the truth."

"Did he happen to say his name?"

"No, don't think so."

"Well, okay, Molly, I really appreciate it. You've given me a lot of good information. Thank you."

"My pleasure, sheriff."

THURSDAY NIGHT FOUND Rick in his cell tossing and turning, like every night since the trial started. He had until Monday to decide whether he was going to take the stand and testify that he was in the bed with Cassie at the time of Marne's murder. Should he sacrifice the future of his marriage to preserve the future of his freedom? Should he sacrifice his freedom to save his wife from knowing that he was having an affair? These questions continued to haunt him throughout the night. Finally, around daybreak when the neighboring cells were beginning to stir with loud, inconsiderate inmates, he made a decision.

He would testify as to where he was on the night of the murder.

He needed to let Kirk Hadley know what he intended to say. Or should he? What if he told Hadley and then changed his mind about testifying, deciding to just let the jury decide the case on the evidence they already had? What if he testified that he was with Cassie but they chose not to believe him, believing instead that he concocted such an alibi, the act of a desperate man trying to keep his neck out of the noose that was closing so tightly around him?

He decided to keep this to himself for just a little bit longer.

JUSTIN PETAKIS WOKE crying on Friday morning, disappointed that the trial of his mother's killer wasn't going forward until Monday, but at the same time at least a little grateful for the break. He had been a bundle of nerves since the trial began, sitting there listening to the testimony of witnesses who described what she looked like when they arrived that night, the condition of her body, how her head had been blown in two with blood splattered everywhere. While he was anxious to see justice done and that animal Rick put in prison where he belonged, he did feel some relief at the thought of having a short break to let the weight of the past few days dissipate a little from his mind.

He was having coffee and rubbing his eyes from the three or four of sleep when his phone dinged. It was a message from his mother.

"You have a video," said the voice coming over the phone.

"Video?" he said to himself. "What video?"

He clicked the prompts on the screen and saw his mother speaking into the phone and videotaping her face as she spoke.

"This is Marne Petakis. Today is Saturday, November 11th and I am hidden in the woods off Armour Road in Jasper County, Georgia. I have suspected Judge Cassie Manson of engaging in some sort of illegal activity where her fines are concerned. I have been given information from my lawn keeper, Sam Echols, that she might be extorting money from people who are charged with certain crimes in her court. He told me that he had a meeting scheduled this morning at seven o'clock with her about her fine, so I have hidden myself in these woods to try to record it. He does not know that I am here and certainly Judge Manson does not know either. I am going to send this video to my son's phone so that it can be activated by him next year, it being my intention that . . . wait. Here she comes."

The phone was turned around to record the road and Marne's voice stopped. A car drove up and parked. A woman got out that he vaguely recognized, a short, pudgy, fat woman with blue jeans that revealed what women call a "muffintop" over her waist. About a minute later a man drove up in a tattered small compact car. He too got out in even more tattered clothes and said, "Hey, Judge."

He watched the video of the two exchanging words back and forth, hearing him refer to her as "Judge Manson," Justin thinking to himself, "What in the world?"

He continued to watch this video, mesmerized, as he saw this man referred to as "Mr. Echols" give money to Judge Manson amid her harsh admonishments toward him. Then he saw her get in her car and speed away, with Mr. Echols doing the same moments later. The video then showed Marne once again, this time with a big smile on her face and excitement in her voice.

"I've got it, I've got it! I knew that bitch was up to something, I just knew it!. I am going to turn this video over to the sheriff, but just in case something were to happen to me that I don't anticipate <chuckle> I am going to send this video to my son, Justin, to pop up on his phone sometime next year. Marne the Magnificent signing off."

Justin sat and stared at the now blank phone screen. After finishing his coffee, he made the obvious statement to himself.

"I've got to get this to the sheriff."

SHERIFF PORTIS DROVE up and parked his car in his usual spot at the sheriff's department. He was about to go into the back entrance when he heard his name called by a man who had also just arrived.

"Excuse me, Sheriff Portis?"

"Yes, sir. Oh hey, Mr. Petakis. What brings you here this afternoon"

"Sheriff, I've got something that's popped up on my phone that my mother apparently sent to me last year in November. I think you should take a look."

"Of course. Please, come inside."

The two went to the sheriff's private office and shut the door. Justin took out his phone and played the video for the sheriff.

"Oh my God, Justin! So it's true. Judge Manson was, maybe still is, shaking people down for money."

"So it's true? What do you mean? Did you know about this?"

"Well, your mother had reported her to me, along with the state court judge and clerk of court, a while back. She said that there are a lot of discrepancies between the fines collected and what the fine totals should be. I had begun to look into it, but when your mother was killed all my attention was diverted to her case and catching the killer. But this really breaks that part of the investigation wide open!"

"What do we do?"

"Well, I need your phone, please. I know, I know, our lives are on our phones these days, but Mr. Petakis, this video is proof positive that Cassie Manson was extorting people out of money. That's about five crimes I can think of just off the top of my head. The district attorney is going to have a field day with this."

Justin handed his phone to the sheriff and was thanked profusely by the lawman.

"I will get my phone back later, won't I, sheriff?"

"I fully intend to return your phone to you in due time, Justin, but this could take a while, as I'm sure you understand. But I'll act quickly, I can assure you that. And again, thank you so much."

"Do you see any connection to this with my mother's murder?"

"Well, that might be a bit of a stretch, Justin. I mean, embezzling is one thing, but I don't really see Judge Manson being involved in a murder. But this is really good proof, concrete proof of her embezzlement. I am so grateful that you told me about this."

SHERIFF PORTIS WALKED into Judge Milton's office with Justin's phone in his hand.

"Hi, Marie. Is the judge in?"

"Yes, sir, sheriff. Just go right in. Good to see you."

"Always a pleasure, Marie."

"Come on in, sheriff. So what's going on with you this morning, my friend?"

"Judge, I've got some earth shaking news. Justin Petakis, Marne's son, brought me his cell phone that had a video sent to it by his mother last November. She had delayed it popping up on his phone until now. I want you to take a look."

The judge's jaw dropped when he saw the video. He could not believe what he was seeing.

"So where are we now? Do you want an arrest warrant?"

"Yes, sir, I do. This is very strong proof of embezzlement. I can't believe that our chief magistrate judge would do such a thing, but here it is."

"Okay. You write the warrant and affidavit and I'll grant it.."

"Thank you, judge."

The sheriff hurried back to his office and wrote out the paperwork for the arrest warrant for Cassie Manson. He submitted it to Judge Milton, who signed it without hesitation. With a deputy in tow he went back to the courthouse and straight to the magistrate office. He found the secretary there, but not Cassie.

"May I ask where Judge Manson is this afternoon?"

"I'm afraid that she has taken the rest of the week off, sheriff. Is there something I can help you with?"

"No, ma'am, I'm afraid not. I have business with the judge herself. Did she happen to say where she was going?"

"I believe that she's in Florida on a short trip, sheriff. She won't be back here until next Monday. I can call her, if you like."

"No, thank you. I have her cell phone number. I will call her directly."

"All right. Let me know if I can be of any assistance."

"Thank you."

The sheriff left the magistrate office and decided not to call Cassie. Let her show back up next week not knowing that anything is afoot.

THE WEEKEND CAME AND went and finally gave way to Monday morning. Rick looked like a man released from a German POW camp in World War II. He was thin, gaunt, haggard, had dark circles under his eyes, walked a little slower than he used to, his voice was softer than it had been before, and he rubbed his temples with his fingers as though constantly fighting a headache. He had thought and thought about whether to testify about being with Cassie at the time of the murder. Finally, he made the final, ultimate decision – he will testify.

Court was called into session and everybody took their seats in the courtroom, this big, spacious room that housed Rick's future. He looked over at the jury and noticed that none of them would make eye contact with him. In just a few hours, or maybe tomorrow or shortly thereafter, he would find out his fate, a fate in the hands of the hostile-looking panel of twelve fellow citizens.

The judge asked if everyone was ready and then said, "Mr. Clinton, call your next witness."

"Your Honor, the state calls Dr. Matthew Brogdon."

Dr. Brogdon took the stand and testified about the condition of the victim. He described how the bullet had torn through her head, ripping it in two, how the jolt of the powerful weapon's bullet had popped her eyeball out of the socket, how half her tongue was missing. He identified the body of Marne Petakis lying on the cold, metal table in the morgue. Several people in the gallery of the courtroom, mostly family members, hurried out of the courtroom during various times during the doctor's testimony, unable to listen to another word. Finally, Jamie Clinton finished his direct examination and Kirk Hadley had none for the doctor.

"Your Honor, the state rests."

"Call your first witness, Mr. Hadley," instructed the judge. Hadley requested a brief recess and the judge, looking at the clock and seeing that it was nearly noon, excused everybody until 1:30, plenty of time for Rick to tell Kirk Hadley his plan to testify and what his alibi would be. They met at the jail and the jailer brought both of them a lunch tray.

"Thanks, I appreciate that," said Hadley. "I didn't expect to be treated to lunch."

The jailer laughed. They had gotten to know each other quite well during his months of representing Rick and his regular visits to the jail, and the jail staff at the Jasper County Sheriff's Department always went above and beyond what was expected of them.

"Well, Rick, what do you want to do? Do you want to testify?"

"Kirk, I've made a decision that's probably going to ruin your appetite. This is going to be the shocker of the year for you, but here it is – I was with Cassie Manson at the time of the murder."

"What? Who? Oh, isn't she the magistrate judge?"

"Yes."

"What do you mean, 'with her'?" Or do you mean what I think you mean?"

"I'm afraid I do. We had been having an affair for some time before the murder, Kirk. I'm not proud of all this, but my head's on the chopping block here. I think I need to testify and let the jury know what really happened that night, at least as far as I'm concerned."

"My God, Rick. You were in bed with the chief magistrate judge when Marne Petakis was murdered? And you're married? Well, I'm your lawyer, not your preacher. I don't make moral judgments about my clients, or judgments at all, for that matter. But Rick, you're telling me the truth, right? You really were having an affair with Cassie Manson and you really were with her the night of the murder?"

"As God is my witness, Kirk."

"Okay then, Rick. That's what we'll go with. I'll call her to the stand first."

"You're going to call her as a witness, a defense witness, a witness for us?! Is that a good idea, Kirk?"

If she's going to lie about this, and I absolutely anticipate that she will, then I want her to look me and the jury straight in the eye and swear under oath that she wasn't with you."

For once, Rick began to feel a glimmer of hope.

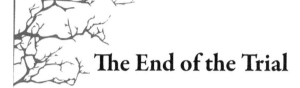

The End of the Trial

Sheriff Portis was in and out of the magistrate office that morning, arrest warrant in hand, but Cassie wasn't there. Her secretary said that she was due in at nine o'clock, but it wasn't unusual for her to take some "personal time" and come to the office much later, often in the afternoon. The sheriff thanked her, walked back out into the hallway and mumbled to himself, "She'd better."

Just as the jurors and others were making their way into the courtroom Cassie Manson stepped off the elevator and turned left to go to her office.

"Sheriff Portis," greeted Cassie. "What a pleasant surprise. How's the trial over there going?" She then walked into her office, the sheriff following closely behind her. Once inside with both the outer door and the door between Cassie's office and her secretary's, the sheriff spoke those devastating words:

"Cassie Manson, you're under arrest for embezzlement." Cassie's eyes widened, then narrowed dangerously. "How dare you!" she shrieked, her face contorting with rage. "Do you know who I am?!" She snatched a heavy law book from her desk and hurled it at the sheriff, who ducked just in time. The tome crashed into a filing cabinet, leaving a sizable dent. "I'm the goddamn chief magistrate judge! You can't arrest me, you stupid son of a bitch! You can't!" Hearing the commotion

Cassie's secretary gasped and slightly cracked the door open, cowering as her boss transformed into a whirlwind of fury. She grabbed her nameplate and flung it across the room, shattering a framed high school diploma, her highest level of education. Glass tinkled to the floor, punctuating her screams. "This is outrageous!" she screeched, overturning her chair with a resounding crash. "I've worked my ass off for this county for years! I deserve every penny and more!" Mascara streamed down her face in inky rivers as she jabbed a finger at the sheriff. "You think you're so goddamn righteous? Ha! I know things that would make your toes curl, Mr. High Sheriff! Things that would turn this town upside down!" She yanked open her desk drawer so forcefully it came off its rails, spilling its contents everywhere. Cassie grabbed handfuls of files, tossing them into the air like confetti. Papers rained down as she ranted, "Everyone's corrupt! Everyone! The whole system is rotten to the core! I'm just the only one with the balls to take advantage of it!" Hyperventilating, Cassie gripped the edge of her desk, her knuckles white. "You want to take me down? Fine! But I'm taking this whole cesspool with me! By the time I'm done there won't be a single 'upstanding citizen' left in this godforsaken town!" With a primal scream that echoed down the courthouse halls, she swept everything off her desk. Her computer crashed to the floor in a shower of sparks, and her "World's Best Judge" mug shattered, spilling cold coffee across the carpet. As the sheriff cautiously approached with handcuffs, Cassie backed away, wild-eyed and feral. She grabbed a letter opener, brandishing it like a weapon. "Don't you touch me! I'll sue you for everything you've got! I'll have your badge for this! I'll . . ." Her tirade was cut short as she tripped over the overturned chair, landing ungracefully on her ample ass with a yelp. The letter opener clattered to the floor and bounced around, sliding under a bookcase. The fight had been drained out of her, replaced by heaving sobs that shook her entire body. "It's not fair," she whimpered as the cuffs clicked into place. "It's just not fair. Everyone does it. Why am I the only one going down?" As the sheriff helped her to her feet, Cassie caught sight of herself in the cracked mirror on the wall. Her carefully crafted image of respectability was gone, replaced by a mascara-streaked, wild-haired harridan. Reality seemed to hit her all at once. "Oh God," she moaned, her knees buckling. "What have I done? My career . . . my life . . . it's all over." The courthouse hallway was silent as Cassie was led away, her occasional hiccupping sobs echoing off the marble floors. Stunned faces peeked out from office doors, watching the spectacle of the once-mighty judge reduced to this blubbering mess. As they reached the elevator, Cassie straightened up, a glimmer of her old defiance returning. "You'll see," she hissed at the sheriff. "When I'm done talking, this whole town will burn. You'll wish you'd never opened this can of worms in the first place."

The sheriff and his prisoner, now a hot mess, stepped into the elevator just feet away from the door of the courtroom where Rick was soon to find out his fate.

Meanwhile, at that same time court eventually resumed for the day, everyone inside unaware of the fiasco going on in the office down the hall. Kirk Hadley's heart pounded at the notion of what he was about to do. Calling a sitting judge to testify as a hostile witness for a defendant charged with murder who places him with her at the time of the murder in a clandestine, immoral, meretricious, adulterous sexual relationship. "My God, what am I doing?" he thought to himself.

But he had a client to represent. He had taken an oath, albeit not very long ago, but he had taken it nonetheless. He was sworn to represent his clients to best of his ability, without passion or prejudice. But right now he couldn't help but be concerned about his own future when word got out in his hometown of Covington that he had called a sitting judge to the witness stand. Would he ever win a case there again? Would the judges there blackball him with their rulings because he had called one of their own as a hostile witness? He had a lot to think about and no time to think about it.

The parties all took their seats in the courtroom. The judge looked out over the courtroom, then at Kirk Hadley and said, "Call your first witness, Mr. Hadley."

"Your Honor, the defense calls Cassie Manson to the stand as a hostile witness."

"Objection, Your Honor," said Jamie Clinton as he quickly jumped to his feet. "This is highly unusual, to say the least. Judge Manson is a sitting chief magistrate judge. Also, I wasn't notified about her as a potential defense witness as is required."

"Your Honor, I learned of her being a potential defense witness literally minutes ago, during the lunch break. I realize this is unusual, but the defendant has the right to call any witness necessary for his defense."

"Well," began Judge Milton, "Mr. Clinton is right. This *is* highly unusual. However, Mr. Hadley is correct too. The defendant is not prohibited from calling a judge to testify if he feels, in his discretion and after careful consideration, that the witness is necessary to his defense. I'll allow it."

The judge turned to look for the sheriff and said, "Sheriff Portis, would you to ask Judge Manson to . . . where's Sheriff Portis?"

"He stepped out, judge," replied one of the deputies. "I'll go out and see if I can find him."

The deputy walked outside the courtroom just as Sheriff Portis was stepping into the elevator with Cassie Manson in handcuffs.

"Sheriff, the judge needs . . . what in the world, sir? Are those handcuffs on Judge Manson?"

"Yes, deputy, they are. I'm taking her to the department. Please call the chief deputy and advise him that I'll be enroute in a few minutes and to be ready for us when we . . ."

"No, sir, I'm afraid that's not possible right now. Judge Milton wants Judge Manson in the courtroom as a witness."

Sheriff Portis stopped and turned around to face the deputy. "A witness?"

"Yes, sir. Bring her into the courtroom, please, sir."

The entire courtroom was taken aback and shocked when Sheriff Portis walked through the glass door with Cassie in handcuffs. The jury looked at her with expressions that could not have been greater had they seen a dinosaur walk into the courtroom. Judge Milton was no exception. He pointed at Cassie and said, "Sheriff, what is the meaning of this?"

"Judge, Ms. Manson is under arrest for embezzlement and violation of public oath . . . so far."

Louise watched this scene from her clerk's chair on the judge's bench in horror.

"Well, uh, she's just been called as a witness for the defense, sheriff," said Judge Milton. "Please remove the handcuffs. Ms. Manson, take the witness stand."

Cassie rubbed her wrists at the removal of the handcuffs, shuffled to the witness stand and sat down, eyeing Rick with a look that, had it been lighting bolts coming from her eyes, would have burned him to a crisp. She gingerly stepped up to the chair and sat down. Louise watched intently from her chair just on the other side of the judge. Kirk Hadley, now with a renewed feeling of confidence, swore her in. She took the oath and wiped her eyes with her trusty tissues.

"Please state your name."

"Cassie Lorene Manson."

"Ms. Manson," he began, "I am Kirk Hadley and I represent Mr. Ambrose seated here at my table. I have some questions for you about the night of Marne Petakis' murder last November. Can you tell this jury where you were that night?"

"I, I don't remember," she said as she gasped for air while crying.

"You don't remember, Ms. Manson? Really? Surely in a little town like this the news of Marne's murder must have been all over the place the next day, or maybe even that same night. Surely you would remember where you were that night when this terrible crime happened and you first heard the news about it. Like people always say that they remember what they were doing when they heard the news that the World Trade Center had been attacked or that former President Trump had been shot. Now I want you to think and think real hard, Ms. Manson, and I'm going to ask you again. Where were you the night of Ms. Petakis' murder?"

Cassie's whole world was crumbling before her eyes. What should she do now? What *could* she do now? Should she tell the truth, a truth that no doubt would exonerate Rick, or keep lying her way through this entire ordeal? But always present in her mind was the first and foremost thought borne of her narcissism – What would benefit her the most?

"Like I said, sir, I have no idea where I was that night. But that being the Monday before Thanksgiving I was probably at the grocery store getting food for the holiday. Yes, that's where I was. I'm sure of it."

"Oh, it was the Monday before Thanksgiving?"

Cassie then realized that Hadley hadn't said anything about what day of the week the murder had been committed.

"Well, yeah, I think that's when it was. Yeah, I'm sure I read that it was the Monday before Thanksgiving."

"Sounds like you knew that already, Ms. Manson."

"I *think* that's when it was, Mr. Hadley. To tell you the truth I haven't thought about it in a long time."

"Which store?"

"Which store what?"

"Which store did you go to that night to get your Thanksgiving dinner groceries?"

"The only grocery store in town, Mr. Hadley."

"Were you alone when you went grocery shopping that night?"

"Yes."

"What time of night?"

"Oh, must've been around nine or ten o'clock."

"Isn't that kind of late to be going grocery shopping, Ms. Manson?"

"Well, I like going when there isn't much of a crowd, Mr. Hadley. I figured the store would be packed during the daytime with it being the week of Thanksgiving."

"Of course. So you went grocery shopping for Thanksgiving, three days away, at nine or ten o'clock at night, by yourself, at the only grocery store in Monticello?"

"That's right."

"So I suppose it wouldn't be much of a task for me to get the security video from the store and see you walk right through the door by yourself at nine or ten o'clock at night on the Monday before Thanksgiving, would it?"

"Well, I suppose it wouldn't, Mr. Hadley, if they keep them that long. That was last year, you know."

"Oh, yes, I know, Ms. Manson. You know, you're probably right. I'm sure they've erased it by now. Anyway, I'll go by there during our next break and ask the manager if he's still got it. Won't hurt to ask, will it?'

Cassie began to sweat even more. More tissues to her forehead.

"Your Honor, would the court entertain a brief break for me to go to the grocery store and ask them if they've got the security video from last November when it was that Ms. Manson testified, under oath, that that's where she was at nine or ten o'clock the night of the murder?"

"Well," replied Judge Milton, "maybe you could just call them in a few minutes, after this witness has testified. I don't mind taking a short break then for you to do that."

"Thank you, Your Honor. I'll do that shortly."

He turned back to face Cassie.

"So, Ms. Manson, are you absolutely, positively certain that you were alone at the grocery store in Monticello on the night of the Monday before Thanksgiving last year at around nine or ten o'clock?"

"Well, you know, Mr. Hadley, that was a long time ago. I believe that I was."

"Oh, so now you're going from being sure you were there to merely believing that you were there. Is it possible that you were not at the grocery store at all that night? Is it possible that you were actually home in bed at that time, and not in bed by yourself?"

Louise stiffened up in her chair as she watched Cassie become visibly more hostile at the tone of the question. "What do you mean by that, Mr. Hadley?"

"Isn't it true, Ms. Manson, that you were in bed with Rick Ambrose, my client and the man seated here at this table who is accused of murder, at the very time the murder was committed? Isn't that true, Ms. Manson? Isn't it?!"

You could hear a pin drop as the jurors glued their eyes to the lady on the witness stand. Louise began to turn pale as she listened to this colloquy from across the judge's bench.

Cassie began to cry uncontrollably. She used the rest of the box of tissues that was on the witness stand and still needed more.

"I don't know what in the world you are talking about, Mr. Hadley. I hardly know Rick Ambrose. He's the husband of my best friend, for Christ's sake! And I never embezzled anything from anyone!"

"I didn't ask you about embezzlement, Ms. Manson. Why do you bring that up?"

"Because that's what the sheriff just arrested me for, goddamnit!"

"I'm not asking you about your embezzlement, Ms. Manson. This is the murder trial of Richard Ambrose only. My sole concern here is Mr. Ambrose's case, not yours. Now, I'll repeat – isn't it true that you were having an affair with Rick Ambrose and you two were in bed together at your house at the time of the murder?"

"Mr. Hadley, I tell you I don't know what you're talking about!" yelled Cassie as she stood up and looked at Rick, then Louise, then back to Rick again.

"You two were having sex in your bed at the time of the murder of poor Marne Petakis, weren't you, Ms. Manson? You two were lying there naked together, arms wrapped around each other, kissing, hugging, making love in the most passionate way, while you weren't the least bit concerned about your supposed friend, Louise Ambrose. Weren't you? Weren't you?!"

"Goddamn you, Rick!" screamed Cassie from the witness stand. "Goddamn you to the depths of hell!" She turned to face Louise and looked at her right through the judge. "To hell with you too, Louise! And Angelina Black too! They were both extorting money from people, just like I was! I didn't do anything they didn't do! And you want to know something else, Mr. Hadley? It was that fucking Harry Blakely who killed her! All I did was pay him to do it! But it was Louise's idea, her idea from the start! She knows it was! She was the one who told me about Harry Blakely, she was the one who got us all into this mess! It was her, her, HER!!! She's the one who got Rick to put his fingerprints on that damn bullet. She's the one who shot his gun to get the empty shell. She's the one who typed up all those fucking letters between him and Marne. She's the one who did all that, not me! Not me!!"

Louise sat for as long as she could and listened, her own anger boiling in her to the point of erupting. She stood up, pointed her finger at Cassie and yelled, "You lying bitch! You goddamn lying bitch!! Don't you say a goddamned word about me! You were fucking my husband and you even came to my office and told me about it!! You were so goddamn proud of yourself!! And you hired Blakely to kill Marne, not me! I never even saw the damn guy after his murder trial! And you're the one who broke into Marne's house and planted those letters in her desk! All this was your doing, not mine! I'm gonna rip your fat face off!"

Louise then lunged around Judge Milton towards Cassie as two deputies rushed to stop her. They grabbed her just as she was about to reach Cassie with a paper weight in her hand.

"Bitch!" yelled Louise. "Bitch, bitch, BITCH! You adulteress! You goddamn adulteress!! You fuck other women's husbands and then complain when you get caught!"

"That's enough, Louise," said the sheriff. "That's enough now!"

The courtroom became as silent as a tomb, the only sound coming from Cassie crying on the witness stand.

Kirk Hadley had done it.

After a pause that lasted minutes but what seemed like hours while the deputies took Louise out of the courtroom the judge calmly said, "Mr. Hadley, do you have any more questions for this witness?"

"No, sir. Nothing further." Rick let out a sigh of relief as he realized there was now no need for him to testify.

"Questions for this witness, Mr. Clinton?"

Jamie Clinton slowly raised his head and said, "No questions, Your Honor."

"You may step down, Ms. Manson."

Cassie walked down the steps from the witness stand with the sheriff waiting for her. He placed the handcuffs on her and led her out of the courtroom. The judge slowly turned to Kirk Hadley.

"Call your next witness, Mr. Hadley."

"Your Honor, the defense rests."

THE CROWD SLOWLY LEFT the courtroom after the verdict proclaiming Rick's innocence of "not guilty" was read out loud by one of Louise's deputy clerks. The sheriff had already taken Cassie to the sheriff's department to have her booked for the crimes she had been charged with and he returned to the courthouse just as the verdict was being read. He smiled as he thought about how justice had been served, had really been served. He stood at the doorway to thank each juror for his or her service. After a short while all of the observers and others left, leaving only a few of those involved in the trial still remaining, buzzing about the trial and congratulating each other on a job well done. Jamie Clinton came over to Hadley's table and extended his hand.

"Good job, Kirk. I must admit, that was a shocker."

"To tell you the truth, Jamie, it was a bit of shock to me too. You did a good job for the state."

"And you for Rick as well, Kirk."

Rick sat sobbing for several minutes then stood, wiped his eyes, took a long drink of cool water from the cup provided by the bailiffs, then poured another full cup and drank it. He grabbed Kirk's hand and thanked him profusely.

"Just doing my job, Rick. Doing what's best for my client. I'm glad it worked out."

Kirk put his papers in his briefcase and headed toward the door where he saw the sheriff standing as if waiting for him.

"Sheriff, that was quite a trial, huh?"

"Mr. Hadley, it was indeed. You did a great job."

"Thanks. So what's next for these uh, public officials?"

"I'm going back to my office to prepare some arrest warrants for Louise Ambrose and Angelina Black. And lest we forget Mr. Blakely. I think I've got enough to go on for now. The rest will be up to Jamie Clinton. But I think that for those four the time to come will be interesting to say the least."

"I suppose it will, sheriff."

"Congratulations. You're a hell of a lawyer, Kirk."

"And you're a hell of a sheriff, David."

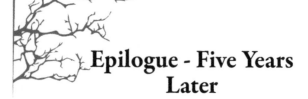

Epilogue - Five Years Later

Kirk Hadley drove up in his new Lincoln Continental to see Rick Ambrose ankle deep in mud in the yard of a house he was grading and seeding for a client.

"Hey there, Kirk! What brings you into this neck of the woods?"

"Oh, I was just passing through here on my way to Macon to meet with a client in a big case I've been hired on down there. I heard you were out this way and I just thought I'd stop by and say 'hello.'"

"Well, I'm glad you did. How have things been going with you? I hear you've got some pretty high-profile cases going on."

"Oh, yeah, the dam pretty much busted after your acquittal. I've had to take on a partner and a full-time secretary. But she's my wife, so don't tell anybody that I'm sleeping with my secretary."

Rick and Kirk shared a heartly laugh. "I'm glad to see that things are going so well for you."

"Thanks, and same here. I hear a lot about your company back in Covington. You've had to take on some more employees, haven't you? And is that a new company truck over there?"

"Oh yeah, I've bought three new trucks. Business has exploded. I've got jobs in Monroe, Jackson, a couple up your way in Covington, one up near Athens . . . I'm running around like a chicken with his head cut off. But the money's pouring in and in the end, ain't that what it's all about?"

"You got that right, my friend. This case down in Macon pays six figures. How're the kids?"

"They're doing well since you did the adoption for me. In school, playing ball, all kinds of things."

"Just curious – you ever hear from Louise?"

"No, not really. I was just as surprised as you were when she consented to me adopting her kids, but I guess she didn't have much choice given her, shall we say, situation. But you know, the kids always thought of me as daddy anyway. I hear her and Cassie are both up for parole again in a couple of years. Don't think they'll get it, though. Conspiracy to commit murder is a pretty serious crime. Same with Angelina. And that guy Blakely, well he's gonna be in prison for a very long time."

"He sure will Well, I'll be on my way. Take care and let me know if you need me."

Rick waved good-bye to his friend and former lawyer, the man who had come through for him at a time in his life when he needed someone to stand by him when all those he was close to had abandoned him. Seeing Kirk brought back the memory of that nightmare from five years earlier and he felt an array of emotions – pain, guilt, anguish, hope, despair, relief. Just as he was mired in his reverie he heard his name being called.

"Hey, Rick, we've got the lawn ready for that seed. What's next, boss?"

THE END

Don't miss out!

Visit the website below and you can sign up to receive emails whenever Tim Lam publishes a new book. There's no charge and no obligation.

https://books2read.com/r/B-A-OZTWB-VAOAF

BOOKS 2 READ

Connecting independent readers to independent writers.

Also by Tim Lam

Timeless Hearts
Ides of Love: A Journey to Ancient Rome

Standalone
Murder in Monticello

Milton Keynes UK
Ingram Content Group UK Ltd.
UKHW030630061024
449204UK00004B/161